ALSO BY SHARON WEBB

Earthchild

EARTH SONG

EARTH SONG

by
Sharon Webb

ATHENEUM

1983

New York

LIBRARY OF CONGRESS CATALOGING IN PUBLICATION DATA

Webb, Sharon.   Earth song.

Sequel to: Earthchild.
"An Argo book."
[1. Science fiction]   I. Title.
PS3573.E212E2   1983   813'.54   [Fic]   82-16298
ISBN 0-689-30964-3

For Bryan

Contents

Acknowledgments

I would like to thank the following people for their technical assistance: Isaac Asimov, Jeff Duntemann, Steve Nesheim, Mike Rogers, George Scithers, R. J. Thompson, Bryan Webb, Tracey Webb, and Jane Yolen. Any errors are solely my own.

I would further like to thank the friends and family members who offered me encouragement and support as I wrote this book.

SHARON WEBB

Mouat-Gari (moo-ä'—gə-rhē') *Abbr.* M-G. 1. A process that confers immortality if begun before physical growth is completed. 2. In a specified year of the immortality era.

    USAGE: In formal usage, M-G precedes the date: *World Coalition colonized the asteroid Vesta M-G 23.*

Heritage Dictionary of the One-Tongue Language, rev. ed., WorldCo Ministry of Education. Chatlanta, M-G 186.

PART ONE

Mouat-Gari

Year 187

Chapter 1

*The silver cobweb hung in the black of space off
Vesta. As Kurt Kraus watched, the distant spincraft
turned, aimed a spidery appendage, and extruded
another shining strand. Tiny one-man Needles, fireflies in the blackness, caught the ends of the strands
and darted with them toward programmed coordi-
nates.*

The web began to curve.

The young aide cleared her throat in an attempt to gain
Kurt Kraus's attention, but the Minister of Culture seemed
not to hear. He had been there for some time, staring outward
from the plex bubble that emerged like a blister from Vesta's
rocky skin. Here at the end of the asteroid's long axis he was
virtually free of the tug from Vesta's slow spin that gave her a
gravity nearly one-third that of Earth.

The aide shifted her position and cleared her throat
again.

Still no response.

She quirked her lip in exasperation. Was he going to stay
there until Dayglow faded? And why did they have to assign
her to an Earther anyway? Especially this one. She had never
been around a minister before. It made her nervous. They
didn't come often to Vesta.

In frank curiosity, she stared at the man's strong profile

3

and searched for differences. The ministers were among the oldest—older than just about anyone in the belt. Some of them were nearly two hundred now.

Well, you couldn't really tell, she thought. But even if they looked like everybody else, they just didn't think the same way. If they did, they'd keep to schedules like they should instead of getting other people in trouble over them. If she let him dememo his schedule and miss the Earth skip, she'd be yelled at for sure, yet she would sooner shrivel than interrupt him. He seemed so intense.

Finally she told herself that she was being silly. She wasn't a child; she was nineteen now—well, almost. And wondering if she would lose all track of time too when she was his age, the girl touched his arm timidly and said, "Mr. Kraus, it's getting late."

The web was an arc now.

So fragile, Kurt thought, so insubstantial.

Another strand of silver thread shot from the spincraft. Needles flashed against the cloth of space in a preordained design so intricate that he saw it as a vast artform.

In the days to come, the web would curve still more; its edges would touch and meld until a spidery egg—a magnificent filigree twenty kilometers across—would hang in the blackness off Vesta.

The spincraft spun its silk; the Needles shuttled—the beginnings of a cocoon that everyone thought was to be a habitat, a mobile mining colony designed to navigate the smaller asteroids and exploit their wealth. Only the Ministry knew its greater purpose.

Kurt's lips moved in soundless words: "For you, Eric." And the dusty lid of memory rolled back and made him a boy again—with a brother. . . .

They lay in sleeping bags under a black Florida sky tattooed with points of silver. "We'll go there someday, Kurt—to the stars."

And he had believed the boy who lay beside him in the soft spring night that hinted of summer.

Kurt blinked at the sudden intimacy of the memory. Eric,

the boy who missed immortality by only a few months, the boy who walked alone leaving Kurt behind to watch him falter into trembling age and infirmity. So long ago.

Kurt stared at the silvery web until he felt an insistent hand on his arm. The pretty little aide said, "You have a meeting, Mr. Kraus."

"So I have." And brushing away her worried look with a smile, he followed her to the Arrow boarding level.

A faint air of hostility followed him. Kurt felt it on the Arrow when it sped him past Dome-Lake Park toward City Central. Nothing overt, just a veiled glance here and there from fellow passengers—a look of curiosity replaced almost instantly with a flat stare, a narrowing of the eyelids, a slightly constricted pupil. He was conspicuous, he knew, in his Earther clothes, his badges of office; equally conspicuous was the hostility toward these things—a hostility that had waxed, then waned for a century and was now in the ascendant.

But it was not overt. It never was.

In City Central, the signs of animosity increased subtly, as if even the airducts breathed it through the halls of Vesta's communications hub.

He dismissed the aide then. She seemed unsure. "I was to see you onto the Earth skiptor."

"I'm sure I can find my way."

With a quick glance as if to gauge his sincerity, or his sanity, she pressed her codex into his hand. "Well then, will you call if you need me?"

He nodded, smiling wryly at the look of relief that spread over her face when the girl realized she was really free to leave.

When she had gone, he walked briskly into Communications Control.

The two cryptists were waiting for him. And there was someone else—a small man with a cherub's face and an elliptical birthmark at the angle of his jaw. The man thrust out a neatly manicured hand in greeting. "Silvio Tarantino, Com Chief."

He took the man's hand, noting the smile that was not

quite echoed in the black eyes. There was something vaguely
familiar about him. "Have we met?"

"I'm sure we haven't," Tarantino said easily. He turned
toward the cryptists. "I've offered to assist your people, but
they seem quite self-sufficient."

"Are you ready to report?" Kurt asked the cryptists. They
were both first-rank technicians on loan from the Prime Minister. Gerstein had said, "If the information is in there, these
two will find it." From the sheaf of print-outs they held, Kurt
felt sure they had uncovered something.

The first cryptist, a man called Crighton, glanced signifi-
cantly at Tarantino, who smiled blandly and said, "I'll leave
you alone, of course."

When the door closed behind Tarantino, Crighton said,
"It took a while to find them. Mallory discovered the key." He
turned to the thin girl next to him. "I'll let her tell it."

Mallory pointed to a series of numbers that were meaningless to Kurt. She read the code easily: first a name, then
age, date of birth, dorm number, and test scores. "This is how
they were hidden." A slim finger ran across the column, "The
child's age was transposed with the dorm number."

"It was a simple trick really," added Crighton, "crude.
And as hard to find as a diamond on an ice floe."

"Cleverly crude," said Mallory. "Slickness would show
deliberate deception. With these results we can't prove it was
intentional."

A knot of muscle moved and ticked at the angle of Kurt's
jaw. So he had been right: children's records had been con-
cealed. "How many? How many have we lost?"

Mallory scanned the printouts, "Twenty-three. Most
from Hoffmeir, of course. Four from Hebe, three from Vesta,
and one from L-5."

"I'd like a translation. Print only. And bio-sketches," he
added.

She nodded, stepped to a console and entered a demand.
In a moment the communicator spit out its text.

He looked at the records in silence. His expression
masked the rising anger he felt. Twenty-three. Twenty-three
lost. A young visiographer—gone now; a mathematician—lost

too; musicians; artists; bright new scientists—all lost forever. Too old now. Beyond calling. Lost over the last three years.

He stared at the print-outs he held and felt their slippery surfaces move under a glaze of sweat from his fingertips. Twenty-three. How many had been as gifted as Jesus Ramirez? How many Tanya Rolfes had been squandered?

And were these all? How many more had there been since he started Renascence? How many more over eighty-eight years?

Two rooms away, Silvio Tarantino's cherub smile twisted into scorn. Did the fools think they could outsmart him? His "crude" trick had served him well for many more years than three.

"How many have we lost" indeed. But one day Kraus would know, wouldn't he? One day he'd realize that the children had been put to better use. Some of them were among his best subjects now.

He looked down at the tiny Listener in his palm. Then, smiling, he stretched out his hand, curling his fingers around the device in a parody of the WorldCo emblem—Earth in a curving, protecting hand.

"Have we met?" he said aloud in a savage mimicry of Kurt's voice. His fingers tightened around the Listener and twisted. Oblivious as its edges cut into the flesh of his palm, Tarantino held just one thought now, a thought he had nurtured since childhood: I don't forget. I don't ever forget.

Mallory handed another sheaf of printouts to Kurt. "We got to these in time. Nine children will make the trip to Renascence."

He took them from her and went through them quickly. Six from Hoffmeir: a dancer, another, a young writer. . . . He stared at the name of the girl: Liss McNabb. Sean's line-child.

He studied the picture of the child. Bright blue eyes stared back. He could almost hear her voice, her quick "Uncle Kurt." Amazingly, she looked like Sean even after generations had diluted his gene pool. Only the bright red hair of the man Kurt called "little brother" was gone—dimmed to soft blonde.

He thumbed through the rest of the sheaf: two from Hebe, only one from Vesta—a boy, David Defour. The boy was a musician, a budding composer.

Kurt stared at the bio-sketch of the child . . . a musician too. Like he had been once—before he had lost his music, before his talent had faltered and finally grown silent. He tried to swallow and somehow found his mouth too dry for it. In some way, the sequence of the day had served to unlock memories that he had thought were safely sealed away forever.

"Will you want to question the Com Chief?" asked Crighton.

Kurt looked up. "No. You two can handle it." He nodded toward Mallory. "As you said, we won't be able to prove anything, but get a statement on record anyway."

Kurt started to hand the print-outs back to Mallory, then stopped. "The Vestan boy—Defour. I want to have a look at him," he said impulsively, surprising himself. He had never done this before, and yet somehow it seemed important. He could not have said just why.

Kurt had not entered a dormitory in over a dozen decades; he had never seen the inside of Vesta's Dormitory Center and yet it seemed to him familiar, as if they were all alike throughout the world, throughout the belt.

"Boys ten to twelve here," said the Mother. "They're in courtyard two now, though. Organized play."

He stepped into the long room and looked at the rows of bed cylinders, each rolled into its dresser stand. Superficially it wasn't like MacDill at all, and yet there was something very much the same. Perhaps the smell, he thought, the smell a room takes when it is inhabited by a dozen boys who have washed with the same soap and eaten the same food and mingled their warm body smells with institutional linens and disinfectants.

He felt dislocated for a moment, as if his life had been dissected into the time he had lived in dormitories and the time before . . . Safety Day . . . the day when the Earth's immortal children were taken into protective custody. . . . He had been fifteen—fifteen years old and suddenly immortal,

suddenly a victim of a band of mortal men who stalked him
. . . a thrown chain cruelly snapping slender ribs . . . the hospital . . . his father with eyes as remote, as cold as space—his
own father saying, "I wanted very much to kill you, Kurt."
The pain of that moment welled up, springing from a deep,
cold place in his soul. He tasted his words again, his bitter
answer to a dying father: "I'm glad you didn't kill me because
I'm going to live. I'm going to live and watch you die."

Safety Day. So long ago, and yet the dormitories lingered
on. He looked across the room at the neat rows of bedrolls,
the boy-battered dressers. Dormitories still, he thought. And
it was better so.

"I'd like to see the boy," he said to the Mother.

"They're in play," she said. "Organized. We don't like to
interrupt."

"From a distance then."

She sighed at the further disruption of her routine and
led him down a wide hallway to a narrow balcony that looked
over a lower-level yard. Below, a group of boys balanced on
bright programmed barriers that moved in rhythm. "Which
one is Defour?"

"There." She pointed to a thin, dark-eyed boy moving
with easy grace through a gauntlet of sliding two-meter-high
barriers studded with handholds. He watched as the boy made
his slow progress: leap, catch, balance, flip . . . leap, catch,
turn, turn.

So young . . . and so serious about it. Kurt felt a sudden
twisting stab of pity for the child. And yet the boy was going
to have a choice—the choice Kurt had never had.

Chapter 2

They brought the boy before the Committee of Vesta when he was eleven years old. His bladder was tense with pressure and it hurt him. Sweat filmed his palms.

The night before, his name had lighted up on the big dormitory board:

DAVID DEFOUR

He'd never seen it there before.

"You're it," said one of the boys with a knowing look that made him feel childish and ignorant.

"I'm what?" His eyes flicked the question from one boy to another to another. "I'm what?"

"You're going to be one."

"Yes," said another.

"You're going to be punished."

"Why?"

"Because."

"Why?"

"Not punished, stupid," said a new voice. "Picked." The new boy, an older boy from upper dorm, put a protective arm around David's shoulder. "They picked you," he said. "You must be special."

"Picked me for what?" But the fear was growing in him, pushing his heart upward to pound and flutter in his throat. He'd heard bits and snatches of gossip before, but he'd ignored it mostly. Now it was coming back to him, but he had to ask it, "What?"

"Why, you'll be fa-mous," drawled the new boy, clutching his shoulder. "You'll have everything you want. But later on—I guess you'll have to die." The boy's eyes sought his. "I wonder what it would be like to die."

David thrust his small body away from the boy's restraining arm and ran on lean brown legs to the bathroom.

He wanted to empty his bladder. He wanted to cry.

It was like that now.

The Committee members, all three, wore their mole-gray robes because they were sitting in formal conclave. The tall square-faced woman who was the Chair touched a glass gavel to the soundpad before her. A tone sounded. "David Defour," said the woman, "approach the Chair."

Fear flickered across his thin face. Legs trembled. Knees wobbled.

"Don't be afraid," said the woman, breaking protocol perhaps because she was kind and perhaps because she remembered what it was like to be eleven and frightened.

He stood before them, looking up at what seemed a great height to the seated members.

The Chair spoke again. "David Defour, do you know why you have been called before the Committee?"

He blinked, pulled in his chin, shook his head almost imperceptibly.

"Is your answer no?"

He summoned his voice, a soprano wavering. "It's no."

"Very well. Member Conway, read the Enlightenment."

Member Conway stared at David with gray steel eyes. Then he looked down and began to read:

"From the first shadows of time, humankind knew that it was mortal. For eons it strived to reach beyond itself. In one sense it failed; in another sense it succeeded magnificently. And always there was the quest.

"The quest led in many directions, meeting success and failure in each. Then humankind found ultimate success— and ultimate failure. Because, when humankind killed death in its laboratories, it killed the need for immortality. When death died, so did the Earth's poetry and its music. Philosophy was stilled; art fell to dust; science was stifled. Only the echoes remained.

"And so it was that humankind realized that great gains reflect great losses. And so it recognized the need to choose from among its members those few who, when denied their immortality, must create it for themselves to the benefit of all.

"It is for this purpose, David Defour, that you have been summoned here this day. . . ."

Member Conway pierced him with a stare. "Do you accept the responsibility with which humankind charges you?"

Cold winds blew through his small body, chilling his belly, creeping into his bones. He stood trembling, large eyes wide, trying to make sense of what he had heard.

The Chair said, "It is customary, David, to say 'I do.' "

His mouth opened, closed, opened again. His voice vibrated in his throat, a captured bee flying out at last. "I do."

"David, I'm here to help ease the transition for you. Do you have any questions?"

He looked at the smooth, bland face across the desk, trying to read it, failing—trying to make sense of the bewildering day, failing again.

After the Committee conclave, he had been taken to Medical Level, helpless, while his body was probed intimately until he felt his face grow hot with embarrassment. Sharp metal removed samples of his tissues, his blood. Then the pronouncement: *Decisional time, sixty lunar months.*

They fed him then, and gave him something to drink. He drank gratefully; the food he pushed around in his bowl. Then he was brought here, to the bland-faced man with pink cheeks and skin as smooth as cream.

"You won't be staying on Vesta, David. Today you'll leave for Renascence. It's on Earth. You'll live there"—he consulted David's record—"for sixty months—until Final Decision." The counselor absorbed the look that passed over David's face. He smiled faintly; he had seen that look before. "You'll like it there, David. Everyone does. You'll prefer it after a time. And at Renascence you'll be with your own kind."

To leave Vesta? The dormitory? Everything he ever knew? He began to shiver. They were going to take him away from his home, from the boys he thought of as brothers, from his bed, from Mother Jacobs and Mother Chin. Hot tears pushed against his lashes, held back only by determined blinking.

And his music. . . . Were they going to take that too? Would he be wrenched away from his flute? His cythar? "Please. Let me stay. I won't be in the way."

"We can't do that, David. Tomorrow, the boys you live with will begin their treatments. The food you eat, the water you drink will be different from theirs. I'm sorry, but you leave today."

A small voice quivering with despair said, "May I take my things?"

"Mother Chin packed for you. Everything is on board the skiptor now." In answer to the dart of hope in the boy's eyes, the counselor added, "It's all there, David. Your musical instruments, too. Especially those. And you'll find more at Renascence. Much more." He rose abruptly. "Now I think we'd better get you aboard. It's a long trip."

"But I can't go yet. I have to say goodbye."

"No, David. We've found that it's better to make the break clean and quick."

He huddled alone in an enclosed compartment in the skiptor. When the door closed, he stared at it bleakly for a few minutes and then gave way to tears.

The flightman, watching his console, took note and wisely let him cry for a while before he pressed the tone button and activated the boy's viewer.

"Hello, David. I'm Heintz. I'll be here to help you through the trip," said the voice from the screen. "If you'll look to the right of your compartment, you'll see a button marked *Water* and another marked *Juice*. I recommend the juice. It's pretty good."

He was thirsty. He pressed the button and a drinking tube oozed out of the wall. It was good. It quenched his thirst.

Heintz waited until the mild sedative had taken effect. Then he said, "Ever ride a skiptor before?"

David shook his head.

"The captain has just come aboard, David. We'll be leaving in a few minutes. I'll tune your screen so you can see departure, but first I want you to engage the webbing. Press the lever in front of you."

A green light came on under his nose; below it, a small handle protruded. He pushed it and gossamer-light webbing emerged from the compartment walls and enfolded him gently but firmly, leaving only his arms free.

"Good. When we're underway, you can disengage on my signal. In the meantime, feel free to explore your compartment. If you want me, press the button over your head marked *Attendant*."

The screen went blank.

Just over his head, a bank of buttons gleamed silver. One said *Music*. He pressed it and a numbered selector presented itself. Indecisively, he pushed a random code and lay back, closing his eyes. The soft strains of a plucked cythar began, followed by the swelling of a senti'cello. An arrangement of a very old piano piece, he thought. What was it? He'd heard it before in his music history class, but the name, the composer, eluded him. The music, inexpressibly sad, seemed to enfold him. He burrowed two brown fists in his eyes to stop the flow of warm tears, but they ran through his curved fingers and traced their way to his chin, as Beethoven's Pathetique played through its silver tape.

A light voice shocked him. "Having a cry? So are all the rest." A sigh. "How boring." A girl about his age peered at him from the visiscreen. Her eyes were frank and blue and a nutmeg sprinkle of freckles dotted her nose. "I hoped you'd be different."

"I'm not crying." He rubbed his eyes vigorously in denial. "I was about to take a nap." He yawned elaborately, sneaking a look at the girl's face. "Who are you?"

"Liss McNabb. What's your name?"

"David. David Defour. Your name's weird. I never heard of anybody called McNabb."

"So's yours."

"Where are you?" he asked.

"Compartment seventeen. You're in eight."

"I thought I was alone."

The girl giggled. "Do you have a vacuum between your ears?"

The giggle made him bridle. "What do you mean?"

"You didn't think the skiptor was making a trip just for you, did you?"

"Well, no—" His chin jutted out just a bit.

"You did." She giggled again.

Who did she think she was, anyway? "Why don't you flash off?" He reached for the privacy button.

"Wait! Don't shut me out. Wait. Please?"

The touch of panic in her voice made him stop, hand on the button.

"Please," she said. "I want to talk awhile . . . I'm lonesome."

He looked at her for a long moment. "Where are you going?"

"Same place you are."

"How do you know where I'm going?"

"I have ways. Wait—Hear that? We're leaving."

The subliminal hum he'd heard since boarding gave way to a heavy vibration that he felt more than heard.

"The bays are opening," she said. "Look."

The girl's face on the visiscreen shrank to a ten-centimeter oval in one corner. The rest of the screen filled with a view of the massive bays of Vesta jutting into hard vacuum. A million star points pierced the black of space.

A lump formed in his throat that wouldn't swallow away. He was really going. Leaving his home—perhaps forever.

"Are you going to cry again?"

He mustered up a scoop of righteous scorn. "No."

"Good. I don't think I could stand that. Watch. We're free."

The last vestige of the bay doors slipped away. Nothing but black and star fire now on his screen—and a ten-centimeter image of a freckle-faced girl.

"We'll be able to disengage webbing soon," she said.

"How come you know so much?" he demanded. He found her annoying and yet at the same time infinitely comforting to talk to, and he didn't quite know where to place his feelings.

"Experience," she said. "I've done all this before."

Skepticism rose. "When?"

"This morning. I was first aboard from Hoffmeir."

"Hoffmeir!"

"Yes. You didn't think they picked just from Vesta, did you?"

He shook his head. He hadn't thought about it at all.

"We stopped next at Hebe. Then we came to Vesta. This is my third departure," she said with the air of a seasoned belt-hopper.

"Oh. How many of us are there?"

"Nine, so far, in the aft compartments. Forward is full of grownups on business trips and vacations. I'm not interested in them. What's your talent?"

"Music."

"I'm going to be a writer. I read all the time. I've even read out of the archives. And I have an enormous vocabulary." She looked at him speculatively. "Most of the music people I've known are inordinately sensitive. Are you?"

He didn't know how to answer.

"I think you probably are, too. I expect you've been sheltered, so I'll try and take you in hand. You'll need somebody like me in Renascence."

"I don't need anybody."

She sighed. "I don't mean to be blunt. I just can't seem to help it. But you seem to be so helpless—"

He shut off the screen for a full five minutes, until loneliness threatened to overwhelm him. He switched on the screen again, thumbing for compartment 17. "Liss?" he whispered. "Liss?"

Her face appeared—freckled, pink and a little puffy around the eyes. Her cheeks showed tear tracks. "Are you going to talk to me, David?" she asked meekly.

"I guess so."

Her chin quivered slightly. "I'm sorry I made you mad."

"It's all right."

"I just say too much. I always have. I don't mean anything by it."

The steady, but almost imperceptible, acceleration suddenly gave way. "Freefall," said Liss.

The compartment light came on as Heintz's voice said, "Passengers may disengage webbing."

David pulled the lever in front of him. Most of the restraining webbing retracted, leaving him with a slightly elastic tether in its place. He found he could move around freely, bounding gently off the padded walls of the little compartment. It quickly turned into a game. One, two (ceiling, wall), three, four (wall, wall), five, six (seat, wall).

He rolled himself into a ball, arms wrapped around his knees. If he pushed off the seat with his toes just so, his rump would impact on the ceiling, aiming him back to the seat. Ceiling, seat, ceiling. A little off center, he caromed toward the visiscreen. Stopped short of impact by the restraining leash, he saw Liss on the screen rebounding too, like a balloon in a wind shaft.

Heintz, watching from his console, chuckled, shaking his head. He'd never encountered a kid who didn't discover that game sooner or later. Natural-born trait, he guessed. He'd never failed to see the aftermath either.

In a few minutes, a slightly green David and a pale and sweaty Liss clung to their seats with one trembling hand while the other reached for the *Attendant* button.

"I'm way ahead of you, kids." Heintz pressed the lever for cabins eight and seventeen, and a cloud of Neutravert sprayed into the compartments. "Take slow, deep breaths." Within thirty seconds, David's nausea was gone, and so was a lot of his starch. "I think I'm going to take a nap now," he said to the image on the screen.

"Me too." And in a moment, "Night, David."

"Night, Liss."

Hands stretching out toward visiscreens as if to touch each other, they slept until time to engage the webbing for the landing on Earth.

They debarked at Atlantic-Biscayne Terminal in the middle of a hot blue morning. David's eyes, dazzled by the cut-glass reflections of the ocean, narrowed to slits. Nearby waves broke over the clear bubble-shields of the shopping centers

and the econdos that had sprung up in the wake of the
man-made island terminal. Miles away to the west, the sky-
line of Miami Beach emerged like a steel oasis from the
sea.

Though it was a hot day, he shivered at the sight of the
ocean. Nothing he had seen prepared him for it, nothing he
had smelled. . . . The odor of the sea clung to his nostrils.
The salt air pressed heavily on his body and seemed to resist
the movement in and out of his lungs. A fine film of sweat
beaded his forehead.

A woman in a blue uniform was saying something.
". . . but you'll acclimate soon. We'll proceed at once to the
hover. We'll arrive at Renascence after lunch."

He saw Liss and moved toward her. She was taller than
he was, bigger than he thought she'd be. Stricken with sudden
shyness, he turned away and pretended to look at the ocean.
After a moment, her hand took his. It felt warm and friendly
to him.

On Earth-heavy legs that shook with effort after a few
meters, they walked the short distance to the zontilator
marked "Hover Boarding."

"This food is guckish," said Liss, wrinkling her nose in
distaste.

He knew what she meant. So far, Earth food seemed wild
and—well, Earthish, compared to his diet on Vesta. And the
water had a taste to it like metal.

"I guess we'll have to get used to it." Liss pushed her plate
away and maneuvered herself into a more comfortable position in the hover seat next to him. Her arm pressed against
his, plump and soft against his bony one. David tentatively
decided that he liked it. He discovered that girls smelled different from boys, and he wondered why he'd never noticed it
before. But then he hadn't paid much attention to girls up to
now. He'd always found them exasperating and not worth
bothering with. And Liss was certainly exasperating, but she
was nice to be around too—in a way. He decided that Liss was
all right. She probably wasn't a typical girl after all. He wondered if all the girls from Hoffmeir were like her.

"What was it like back home?" he asked.

"You mean compared to Vesta? Well, Hoffmeir is much smaller, of course, and newer, as you might expect of a man-made habitat, but we live inside just like you did on Vesta. And the people of Hoffmeir are ever so much more intelligent."

He faced her in surprise, pushing away her plump little arm in the process. "What are you talking about?"

"It's true. Everybody knows that Vestans are just technicians. There's variety on Hoffmeir. Why, the university alone is the best in the system. It says so in the archives. Besides, in a small, select society like Hoffmeir, there's a premium on brains."

She'd almost had him fooled. She was a typical girl all right. In fact, she was so typical she was outstanding. He bet Hoffmeir was full of space-brained girls just like her. His voice dripped scorn, "I bet anyone in my dorm is twice as smart as you."

"You lived in a dorm?" Her eyes widened, then crinkled at the corners. "Oh, of course."

"What do you mean, 'of course'? Where did you live?"

"With my parents."

He felt his mouth drop open. "Lie." She really must think he was stupid to believe a story like that. Nobody knew his parents until the day they welcomed him into the community of adults. A two-year-old would have better sense than to tell such a tale.

"It's not a lie. I knew Vestans weren't so intelligent, but you're proof that they're stupid."

"I'm stupid!"

"Yes, you are." She fumbled at her belt and drew out a little holo cube. "Look at it."

He thumbed the light on. A smiling man and woman sat at a table decorated with green Renewal Day light cubes. A girl—Liss—entered, carrying a ceremonial vinifountain. She set it down before them and the tall man drew three drinks from it. Their hands raised in a formal toast.

A three-dimensional greeting floated by:

> *To our daughter on this day of rejoicing.*
> *May she find her way, and well.*

David stared at the holo in disbelief.

"Now do you believe me?"

"I don't understand—" he began. "Why . . . How do you —" He stopped, not knowing how to phrase all the questions in his head. Only officials and a handful of others were allowed to reproduce themselves to begin with, but they never raised the child themselves. It just wasn't done. Finally, he said, "They must be very important."

"They are." She drew her shoulders back slightly. "My father painted the official portrait of Prime Minister Gerstein. There have been artists in my family since my great-grandfather, Terry McNabb. He was one of the first children to go to Renascence. And my mother is poet-laureate of the belt—including your precious Vesta."

One eyebrow rose, questioning. "Then, if they do that, that means. . . . That means—"

"Yes," she said. "They're mortals."

The hover suddenly plunged below the cloud cover. "Look!" Liss's nose pressed against the curving window followed quickly by David's. A rumpled green rug of mountains stretched below them.

The hover swooped between two mountains, skimming through a narrow pass, dipping again, following a silver curving streak that plunged down a stony gorge, finally leveling in a wild, wooded valley.

David felt giddy with the flight and slightly drunk with exhilaration. Nothing he'd ever experienced, not freefall in the skiptor, not anything compared to it.

The hover dropped again, barely missing the treetops. The silver streak became a river bounding over the rocks in its path. Ahead, the trees thinned to a small clearing. The forward rush of the hover ceased as it began its gentle vertical drop.

There were people waiting for them.

The man who had taken him in tow said, "We want you to rest today. Rather than gather you all together to listen to boring speeches, we've arranged private orientations."

They were walking along a winding gravel path through deep woods. Alongside, a bright stream jumped from stone to stone, gurgling and chuckling its way to the river. Here and there, small wooden buildings sprouted like brown mushrooms under the trees.

The effort of walking, of drawing breaths from the heavy air, was almost too much. He felt his knees buckle. A firm hand caught him, steadied him. "Here we are." The man pushed open the door to one of the little units.

The cabin was a single room with a tiny bath just off one end. A bed cylinder lay rolled against one wall. The man pushed a lever and it opened. "Rest awhile, David. Later"— he indicated the communications bank against the opposite wall—"you'll learn more about Renascence. After you've rested, someone will come to take you to dinner."

The man smiled and ran a large hand through the boy's hair. "I know how confusing it is, David. I know how you feel."

He looked up in surprise and disbelief. No one could really know how he felt.

The man looked at him, but it was as if David weren't there at all for a moment. Then he said, "This was my cabin, too. Twenty-two years ago."

He was too tired, too unsettled, to sleep. Like a wooden thing, he lay on the little bed and looked dully around him. The windows were open and the warm, heavy air pressed into the room bringing strange smells and sounds. Once a bird called, and he started at the sound of it, trying to catalogue it in his mind. The only birds on Vesta were the chickens and ducks of Sustenance Level, and the empty holo images from Education.

The sunlight, coming through the window, laid a rectangle like dusty yellow chalk in the center of the room. In the rectangle stood a graceful music stand with manuscripts arranged on it. His own cythar and his flute sat next to the stand. He felt grateful for them, as if they represented a continuity in his life.

Across the room, attached to the communications bank,

was a triple keyboard. Did it have amplifier bars? Curiosity propelled him to his feet and across the room. Amplifier bars. He couldn't believe it. There was only one symphosizer on Vesta that could compare with it. His own—the one they'd let him use—was like a toy compared to this one.

He stood before it, fingers poised, afraid to touch it, but tempted beyond redemption. He pressed the control marked "soloboe," and played a fragment of melody that had run through his head for a while. The symphosizer echoed in a plaintive reedy voice. "Remember," he said under his breath, pressing the *store* control. The bassoon was next, no—two bassoons—rollicking drolly in the lower registers. "Now. Together." The trio echoed in the little room. David, listening critically, pressed *delay*, then the code for bassoon I and II. "Repeat," he said to himself. Better, he thought, dark eyes shining at the sound filling the cabin. Better. He stored it all, marveling at the intricacies of the symphosizer. It could cut out dozens of mechanical, uncreative steps. No more delays between the idea and the realization.

He activated the bassoon voices again, playing one against the other in an argument. The voices rose, and he giggled at the strident duck squawks. Now a chase . . . A crash. A cartoon ending—two irate bassoons with duck mouths—tumbling over and over each other, protesting wildly until they were out of breath, their squawks subsiding to disgruntled, infrequent quacks.

An idea came. He held the sensor to his throat and subvocaled, "Duck-eater, duck-eater, duck-eater, duck-eater." He pressed an amplifier bar, sighing it . . . *d-u-c-k-e-a-t-e-r.* Now, chop it . . . *d'd'd'd'K—e—a—t—e—r.*

He played with the controls until he had his monster galumphing after the bassoon ducks. It started with a flat-footed walk in the lower registers: *D'D'Kuh.* Ominous. He keyed in the ducks in a low-pitched quack.

D'D'Kuh, D'D'Kuh.

Then a sighing, *e—a—t—t—t.*

Roll it down seventeen tones: *E—a—t—e—r-r-r!*
D'D'Kuh.

Nervous duck quacks, and then the chase: *D'D'Kuh. E— a—t—e-r-r-r KUK---smeer-PING.*

It ended with a deliciously horrible duck scream and the monster's sighing, *E---a---t--t--t*.

Visions of swirling duck feathers floated in his head. Tickled at the image he'd evoked, he laughed out loud.

"Good afternoon, David," said a male voice from the communicator.

Startled, he looked up.

"We're going to begin your orientation now. Watch the viewer, please."

As he stared at it, the image of a large, dark man came on. The voice said, "You were brought here at the direction of this man, Citizen Kurt Kraus, Minister of Culture." David shivered involuntarily.

The image of a satellite map was next. "The skiptor landed here. . . ." An enlargement of the map, then the scene at Biscayne-Atlantic. "You boarded the hover and arrived here." The green mountains appeared—pinpointed on the satmap. "You are in an area known as the Blood Mountain Wilderness, part of the North American continent once known as Georgia. The wilderness area is over 4000 square kilometers, of which Renascence is allowed the use of 180 square kilometers." The image focused on a small area.

David recognized the brown cabins near the landing site.

"You are here, in dwelling six."

Actual images gave way to a stylized map showing study center, dining halls and a large recreational lake. At the edge of the lake a series of performance halls were displayed.

"You'll soon learn your way around, David. Now, we want to tell you a little about Renascence. You were brought here, as were the others, with very little information about this operation. That is the way it was planned. We want each of you to discover for yourself what our life is like. Although your arrival was abrupt, and your discomfort acute, it has enabled you to look at your new life without preconceived attitudes and prejudices.

"We live a simple life here. Simple, but enriching. You will find complexity enough in your work and in the interactions with your teachers and your peers. This, too, is deliberate. We have sought to form an environment conducive to creativity, and one which, we hope, simulates an earlier, simpler time when all humankind faced an abbreviated life span.

"While you are here, you will learn more than the discipline of your art. At Renascence, you will learn a reverence for the ideas and the cultures that humankind has pursued throughout its history.

"Each of you has received a Final Decision time. In your case, David, the time is sixty lunar months. In sixty months, if you decide not to remain with us, you may make your Final Decision for immortality treatments. Beyond that time, your body will have matured too much for treatments to begin.

"We, of course, hope that during your stay here you will choose to remain. However, if you decide to leave us, there will be no reproaches, and no disgrace whatsoever.

"You will be meeting your teachers soon, David. If you have questions, the communicator will answer them."

The voice fell silent.

A sharp tap on the door, and then it opened. "I'm exploring," said Liss closing the door behind her.

"How did you know where I was?"

"Easy. I asked the communicator. Come here and I'll show you where I'm staying." She pointed out the window to the creek, nearly hidden beyond a clump of dark, graceful trees. "See those trees? The communicator says they're hemlocks. Anyway, just beyond, there's a little footbridge. After you cross, there's a path right to my door." She giggled. "It's a little like the witch's house in Hansel and Gretel, don't you think?"

He looked at her blankly.

She searched his face and sighed. "Don't you know anything about mythology?" She shook her head. "Technicians. Well, I'll just have to take you in hand and—" She stopped. "I'm doing it again, aren't I? I'm sorry. Please don't squinch your face up at me like that. It gives me the wooly-woolies."

She seemed so distressed, and so sincere, he felt his face relax and a smile grow there. "All right."

"I really would like to tell you about Hansel and Gretel though. That is," she added quickly, "if you want to hear it."

"Well, go ahead then."

"Oh, not now. Tonight. It's a bedtime story. Show me your things," she said. She pointed to the symphosizer. "What's that?"

He told her how it worked.

"Interesting," she admitted. "Then you can work two ways just like I can."

"What do you mean?"

"Well, my cabin has a processor on the communicator. I can use that to write, but in the middle of the room, about where that music stand of yours is, sits the funniest thing. It's a tall piece of furniture with a slopey top. And it has a stool drawn up to sit on."

"What are you supposed to do there?" he asked.

"Write." She watched for his reaction, giggling when the puzzlement spread over his face. "There's a stack of paper and pens on the desk. Can you imagine something so primitive? I asked the commicator about it. Did you know that in the olden days lots of writers actually wrote that way?"

He shook his head.

"I think I might try it. It's rather romantic, don't you think? Anyway, I see that you have the same arrangement here." She walked up to the music stand. "What's this?"

David examined the sheets. Some were blank except for the musical staff printed on them. Others were compositions for cythar and for flute.

"How does this sound?" asked Liss, picking up a sheet at random.

He looked at it in surprise; it was titled "David's Song." The composer was somebody called T. Rolfe. He fitted his flute together and began to play, slowly at first, for it was a difficult piece, then faster, more fluently as he began to feel the mood of the music.

"That's beautiful," said Liss as he finished.

"I agree," said the woman at the door, who had entered unnoticed. "I can't imagine it played with more feeling."

David looked up with a flush of pleasure. The pleasure died when he saw her, and cold things crept on spider legs in his belly.

The woman was old. Old in a way that David had never

seen. She was small and stooped. Wise dark eyes burned from a face encased in wrinkled, wilted flesh. Her hair fluttered in wild gray-white strands around her head. Sagging skin made jaw and throat a continuous webbed mass. He shuddered.

"I heard you playing the song I wrote for you," she said, "and so I stopped in. I'm going to be your teacher, David."

While he stood dumbly by, Liss said, "Oh, then you're T. Rolfe."

"Tanya."

"Will David learn to write music like you?"

The old woman smiled, increasing tenfold the wrinkles wreathing her face, cornering her mouth and her eyes. "We'll see."

When she'd gone, David still stood silent, contemplating the apparition of age.

"She's nice," said Liss. "Don't you think so?"

He looked at her, stricken. "She's . . . She's ugly."

"She's just old," said Liss. "She must be nearly a hundred."

Nearly a hundred! Smooth-faced Mother Chin at his dormitory was nearly a hundred and fifty. Mother Jacobs was older yet. He felt his jaw clench. "How can they do it? How can they?"

She touched his shoulder, patted it. "I'm sorry. I forgot. You've never seen mortals before, have you?"

He shook his head miserably. Then he looked at her for a long time. "You're not afraid of it, are you, Liss?"

Surprise flickered over her face. "Why, no. I guess I'm not. And now," she said briskly, "I suggest we investigate supper. I expect it will be guckish, but right now, I don't even care."

Later that night, he lay alone in his cabin, as miserable and skittish as a pup away from its litter mates for the first time. Far away, an owl called. Nearby, another answered. Startled, he sat up, looking through the window into deep shadows and moonlight. Nothing stirred.

Uneasily, he lay back. He wanted to be home, tucked into his bed in the middle row between Jeremy and Martin, lulled by soft snores and muffled sleep sounds. He wouldn't stay here. He wouldn't. Not even if they tortured him.

Slowly exhaustion and sleep overtook him.

He dreamed of walking alone in brooding woods. After a time, he knew that he was lost. He panicked and began to run until he came to a clump of trees and a footbridge over the creek. His feet thrumming on the little path, he ran, calling, "Liss. Liss." The door to the cabin—the wicked witch's house —fell open. Tanya Rolfe stood in the doorway beckoning with hands like claws.

He stirred and muttered in his sleep. Outside his window an owl swooped on silent wings, its talons pinioning a small gray mouse.

Chapter 3

Kurt Kraus glared at the image of the Minister of Population. "Renascence is not a wastebasket."

"Genetically, it may be," said Ndebele. "When you allow indiscriminate breeding without prenatal determination of fitness, you are bound to have defectives."

Kurt felt the anger burn in him. He masked it carefully. "Who is to say what makes a human 'fit'? Is the Ministry of Population the final word on 'fitness'?" He put a faint stress on that word "fitness," an enunciation that served to make the word, and the idea behind it, distasteful.

Muntu Ndebele leaned back in his chair and looked down his elegant nose. "In this case, I think it is." With his palm upward, he stabbed a long index finger in Kurt's direction. "Item: Point four six percent of the population of Hoffmeir demonstrate marked physical or mental aberration." His second finger joined the first. "Item: All but point oh one of the Hoffmeir defectives resulted from a union of Renascence mortals." The third finger moved into place with the other two. "Item: Genetic control among immortals on Hoffmeir has resulted in a vanishingly low rate of defectives." The little finger flicked from its restraining thumb, "Item: Genetic control among Renascence mortals is nonexistent." And then the thumb, "Three percent of Hoffmeir's population is mortal. And that three percent is responsible for nearly all the defectives."

Item, thought Kurt. You are an ass, Ndebele. Aloud he

said, "That's true. Genetic control among Renascence mortals is nonexistent. And I intend for it to stay that way."

"There is no excuse for this situation. None."

"No?" Kurt smiled thinly. "What about your own existence? Are you aware that one half of the team that discovered the immortality process was a 'defective'? Frederick Gari was a dwarf, and until he was ten years old he was considered retarded."

"We're not discussing Gari here."

"I think we are. How many like him have you caused to be aborted?"

"You deal in theory. I deal in absolutes. You have allowed point four five of the population of Hoffmeir to be born defective."

"Then that's my problem."

"Not yours. Mine. That population is growing, thanks to Renascence. And as these defectives reach the age of physical maturity and become immortal, it becomes society's problem, Kraus. For eternity."

Kurt's face remained placid except for the lump of muscle that ticked at the angle of his jaw. How was he supposed to deal with a man who used statistics instead of brains? "The mortals of Renascence have given up their eternity for the good of us all. Part of the bargain is the guarantee that they can reproduce themselves."

"No one is denying that bargain. It's a matter of control."

Kurt shifted slightly to the right of the imager's focus and leveled his gaze at the Population Minister—an old trick, but useful. In Ndebele's office, Kurt's gaze would be slightly askew, enough to be disconcerting. "Forty years ago a boy without legs, a son of mortals, made his Final Decision. He gave up his immortality. And that boy was Jesus Ramirez, the man who developed the theory that is responsible for the Ramirez Star Drive. Because of this 'defective', human beings will be able to travel soon to the ends of the galaxy."

Ndebele's eyes shifted uneasily. "Frankly, it's not those types that concern this office. Most of those children opt for mortality." He paused, then said, "We are most concerned with the incidence of mental retardation. Those children leave Renascence and enter the general population."

So that was the crux of it. Kurt stared at Ndebele and waited for the rest.

"Population expects a prenatal determination in each case, with abortion of all mental defectives."

"Population can go to hell."

"We expected this reaction," said Ndebele. "Therefore, Population intends to refuse housing for all mental defectives born to mortals."

"Refuse housing!"

"Exactly. You'll have to keep them at Renascence."

"We have no facilities for their care. For their training."

"That can be arranged."

"In other words, you propose to deny them the process," said Kurt slowly. "You propose to leave them at Renascence until they die."

"It's for the best," said Ndebele.

Kurt's narrowed eyes blurred the man's image into a wavering ebony column. Gradually he focused again on the arrogant Minister of Population. No, he thought, I won't let them die.

Somehow his whole life seemed to be inextricably bound to mortals. He had seen them age and sicken, seen them die. He had been responsible. Part of him was diminished with each death. And yet, he believed in Renascence and in what it had accomplished. He would not see it profaned. When he spoke, his voice was cold. "I think not. I don't accept your solution. And I'd like to remind you that this office is the sole determinant of which children Renascence accepts." He shifted back toward the imager and stared directly into Ndebele's eyes. "All other children—all others—remain your responsibility."

He watched the Minister's face contort in anger. So, he had won the first game. Uneasily, he wondered who would win the second.

Chapter 4

David Defour stared at the corrections Tanya Rolfe had made on his composition. It wasn't any use. In the three years he'd been on Earth, he'd never gotten back a score without those hated corrections. He crumpled the sheets in his hand and threw them to the floor.

The old woman shook her head slowly. "David. David. You are here to learn. You *are* learning, but you are like a young plant not yet grown. It's too soon to expect a harvest."

Too soon, always too soon. He waited for her next line.

"You must crawl before you can walk, David. Walk before you can run." The old woman looked at him sharply, then she laughed. "You hate my platitudes nearly as much as my corrections."

His chin jutted defiantly.

"Oh, David. You're always so impatient. We can only lay a foundation here. Your music has to grow—to mature as you mature. It may take a lifetime before you compose something of enduring value. Perhaps longer. Perhaps never."

She touched the communicator controls and received another print-out of his piece. "Let's start again, David, from this measure. Now this is a good beginning, but you take it nowhere. . . ."

He heard her voice going over the piece, but her words didn't register. What she'd said before kept repeating itself in his brain.

Half a lifetime. Perhaps longer. Perhaps never.

Chapter 5

As Dayglow faded, twinkling lights began to appear on the upswept horizon of Vesta. A crowd had gathered on the green of Dome-Lake Park. Nearby, the Arrow decelerated, stopped, and disgorged another load of passengers.

Silvio Tarantino sat alone in the small green room and looked out at the people gathering below. He leaned back, satisfied at the crowd, and waited for the ceremony to begin. It would be an hour before his appearance. The bulk of his speech was taped—a carefully orchestrated tape that had taken him two days and half an intervening night to prepare.

He stood and looked at his image in the reflector. He wore new clothes—the formal cloth of office—and on his left breast the ribbons of the Ministry.

He poured himself a glass of wine and then sat down again in the dimness of the room. A silence. Then the muttered drums of ceremony.

He watched the tape on a small three-vee that emerged from its niche on the opposite wall.

Outside on the green, the silent crowd watched too, and there, the figure of Silvio Tarantino was larger than life. Much larger.

The tape was being broadcast throughout the asteroid colonies and to the people of L-5 circling the earth.

He sipped his wine. The figures moved and spoke: Prime Minister Gerstein clasping his hand, pinning the ribbons to his chest, clasping his hand again, calling him "Deputy Minister."

As Gerstein spoke, a shadow fell below his eyes, making them seem shifty, making them seem less open, less honest. The shadow moved into the crowd's mind at once, and its subconscious, as efficiently as a computer, enhanced the shadows and read the meaning:

$$H \; y \; P \; O \; C \; R \; I \; T$$

As the tape ended, the lights of the colony began to dim. A single voice, chosen for its timbre, began to sing the anthem of the colonies, "Lone Pioneers." The voice sang without accompaniment at first. Then, gradually, faint drumbeats began and grew to a mutter, then a martial call.

As the song ended, the drums faded to a whisper. And as the whisper insinuated itself into the minds of the people, the lights blinked out. Vesta was dark.

The people on the green looked at blackness. Straining eyes dilated at nothing. There was no sound but the insistent whisper of the drums.

A stabbing blaze of light exploded in the crowd.

The people gasped at the brilliance. And when they could focus, they saw that their new Deputy Minister stood before them, with head thrown back and arms outstretched as if in ecstasy. And they smiled at this, and nodded one to another, as drumbeats muttered in their minds, *Silver T, Silver T . . .*

Chapter 6

David tapped at the door of Tanya Rolfe's cottage. There was a sound of chair scraping against floor, then a voice, "Come in."

The wrinkled face moved in a smile. "Good morning, David. I've been expecting you to come by to see me."

"But how? Today isn't my lesson."

"No." The dark eyes looked at him keenly. "But most of my boys and girls come when they reach this point. Come and sit with me, David. Have a cup of tea." She took his firm hand in hers, drew him to a chair, and poured strong tea from a thin old china pot.

The odor of sassafras and lemon rose from the cup. It seemed to him as he sipped from it that Tanya Rolfe was like her teapot—crazed and fragile with age, but filled with good strong stuff that warmed him.

"You are sixteen now. Your Final Decision is not far away."

He nodded. "Tomorrow."

"So soon?" She sighed deeply, her breath running out in reedy tones. "I thought a month, perhaps, or two. So soon." A veil seemed to come over her eyes for a moment, a fleeting look of vulnerability.

He wondered that he'd missed it before. How had he missed seeing how fragile she'd become the last few years? Her hand on the cup was translucent porcelain, patterned with thin blue veins. In dismay, he realized that he'd not really

seen her before. He hadn't heard the faint rattle of air as it
moved in and out of her lungs. Hadn't noticed the swelling of
instep and ankle above her tiny feet. Hadn't seen the effort in
her movements. He clenched his fist, feeling nails bite into
his palm.

She set down the cup and took his hand in hers, opening
it, relaxing the curved fingers. "You want to know what will
happen to your music if you decide to leave us."

He nodded, staring at their twined fingers, at her heavy
gold ring.

"You're a highly skilled musician, David. You have tech-
nique that can improve with time and maturity. You have
talent, too. You're musical. But you have something
more. . . ." She paused, looking through the window at something that lay far beyond the scope of her eyes. "It's something
called 'The Divine Discontent.' I think of it as a yearning
to move outside of myself—to be a part of something
more, something greater, and yet to still be uniquely Tanya
Rolfe.

"It's the discontent of a sapient wave lapping on a beach,
shifting the sands, and knowing that when it is gone, another
will wipe out all traces of its path. And it feels rage—" A touch
of passion edged her voice. "Rage." Then she laughed softly.
"Some call it the thumbscratch syndrome."

He looked at her, puzzled.

"We're transients too. Like the waves, our comings and
goings change the face of the earth. But it isn't enough. We
feel the need to personally scratch the face of eternity—deep
enough to leave a scar. Proof, you see, that we've been here."

"And if I'm always going to be here?"

"Then, there goes your motivation. Immortality is a sure
cure for the thumbscratch syndrome."

"But if I did—"

"You'd still be clever, David. And competent. But you'd
be striking a cooling iron. And after a while, it wouldn't matter
to you."

He nodded, stood, walked to the door, then turned. "Has
it always happened like that? Is it for sure?"

"I can't say that the spark must go out. But it always has,

David." Her hand, gentle as a moth, touched his shoulder. "It always has."

He moved up the hill, feeling his leg muscles strain, feeling his breath come in short gasps. Sunlight, filtering the new leaves of May, dappled the spongy forest floor beneath his feet.

He sought a high crest, a place where he could overlook Renascence. He wanted to see it all, for once. If he could see it all, maybe he could make it fit together in his mind.

He stepped over a rotting tree trunk in his path and froze. Glittering death coiled by his foot. He heard the warning rattle with only part of his brain. Another part observed, actively orchestrating his fear . . . a rattling maraca: a tom-tom mimicking the beat of his heart. Accelerando. Silence. A silence whimpering in his mind at 440 cycles per second—increasing to a scream—ten thousand cycles, twenty, more. Pulsating beyond the audible range. Felt.

If it struck, if its fangs entered a vein, an artery, he was too far from help.

His muscles contracted. He sprang, running through the open woods to a raucous brass accompaniment in his head, running with a tom-tom throbbing against his chest, his throat.

Had it struck? Would he feel it, if it had?

Reason told him he was safe; fear thrust him ahead. His muscles propelled him on. He ran until his body rebelled and withdrew his strength and his breath. He fell in a heap at the foot of a wide oak, leaning his back against it for support.

"Coward," he said aloud to himself when he had breath. "Coward." But part of him rankled in defense. What else could he do? He didn't want to die.

He didn't want to die.

He made his way back down the mountain to the stream by the clearing. A tall reed-thin boy pressed wet clay in spiraling shapes on a flat stone emerging from the shallow water. He looked up. "Ah, David. Been up the mountain?"

It was more than a casual phrase. Sooner or later, nearly everyone made that trek alone—as if it were a biological need like food or water, as if the mountain held answers that the valley couldn't. David nodded. "Been up the mountain, M'Kumbe."

"Does the air breathe softer there?" The tension in the question revealed itself in the long black fingers kneading the slick clay.

He didn't know how to answer.

The black eyes looked into his, the fingers moved. "I build my own—here." The lump of clay rose against the pressure of the boy's hands and grew ridged like a naked spine against the rock. "It rises, it falls. I can be a god to this little mountain. But in the end, it's only clay." He brought down his fist, smashing the earthen spine. Then he smoothed it into a flat cake, blending it with pale pink palms and long black fingers, bisecting it with a curving "S." "Up and down. Yin and yang." The fingers stopped for a moment. "Liss is looking for you. She's looked all morning."

He found her in her cabin, sitting on the old tall stool in front of her desk, writing.

"A poem?" he asked.

"A letter. To myself." She wrote a few moments longer, then laid the pen down and looked up. "It's a thought-straightener."

"Three people told me you wanted to talk to me."

"I do. But right now, let's walk." She slipped off the stool and picked up a small split oak basket that sat in the corner of the room. "The blackberries are out." She swept out of the cabin and was halfway over the footbridge before he caught up with her.

"What's wrong?"

"Nothing." She looked at a point just over his head as if she found it of utmost importance.

He took her shoulders, turning her toward him. "What's wrong, Liss?"

She twisted the little basket from side to side in her hand. "Nothing. I've just developed a love for blackberries." Her chin thrust defiantly, but she avoided his eyes. "I like them so well, in fact, that I've decided I want to eat them forever."

His hands slowly dropped to his sides. He leaned up

against the railing of the little bridge, trying to think. Of all the people here, Liss had been the most sure.

Her lips turned up at the corners, but her eyes didn't match. "There's an old saying, David: 'It's a woman's prerogative to change her mind.' Ever heard it?"

He shook his head.

A slight crinkle grew around her eyes. "Technician." And then the old joke, "I'm going to have to take you in hand."

They began to walk. They walked for quite a while before they came to a rambling patch of blackberry bushes, before he said, "Why, Liss?"

Her hands flew among the leaves, picking soft, ripe berries, staining the basket and her fingers purple. Without answering, she reached for a cluster deep within a bush and, with a little cry, drew out her hand, empty. A deep scratch curved across the skin, and tiny drops of blood appeared here and there, merging into a red line. She began to cry, all out of proportion to the hurt, shoulders heaving, little snub nose turning red and snuffly.

He watched her, feeling utterly helpless.

The basket fell to the ground, spilling berries into the grass, and still she cried, curving her hands into fists. And then, between breathless, racking sobs, she said, "Don't you know anything? Don't you know *anything?*"

He stood accused, not knowing of what.

"Technician." She drew in a huge snuffling breath. "You're supposed to comfort me. It says so in all the books."

Dismayed, he reached out awkwardly and patted her head, ruffling her soft hair under his fingers.

Unaccountably, she began to laugh. It started halfway between a giggle and a gasp. Then it grew to madhouse proportions, until she had to sit down in the warm new grass. It was infectious and he found himself on the ground beside her, laughing too. Hugging her, laughing, then kissing in a heap of scattered blackberries. And it seemed to him then that maybe they were both crazy, but it didn't matter.

Tossing their clothes in a purple-stained tangle, they clung together, rolling on the soft warm ground, pressing together with cool flesh and frantic need. Later, laughing, they ran naked down the path to the lake and plunged into the frigid, heart-stopping water.

After they dressed, they walked in the sunlight, briskly at first, trying to warm up. They took the high path back along the broad back of a ridge. Below them, they could see the clearing.

In the sharp blue sky, a line grew to the shape of a disc. "Look," said Liss. "The hover. Let's watch."

The hover stopped its forward surge and dropped gently to the floor of the valley. The doors opened, disgorging a cargo of seven children.

"Do you remember the day we came, David?"

He nodded, watching the little group. One boy stood apart from the rest, shoulders back, legs slightly apart, looking braver than he could possibly feel. Another looked around with eyes as big as the landscape he tried to take in. They seemed so little.

She echoed his thoughts. "Were we ever that small?"

"I suppose we were."

"It must have been harder for you," she said. "You were plucked out of a dormitory and brought here. I never lived that way—there were just me and my parents. I was used to being alone back at home. But, you know, I think you did better than I did." She sat down, drawing her arms around her knees. "I've found out that I need people around me. You found out that you didn't."

He felt an eyebrow raise.

She laughed, crinkling her nose at him. "Well," she said coyly, "sometimes you need people. But most of the time you're buried in that cabin of yours like an ingrown nail in a toe."

"Is that your poetic opinion?"

"It may not be poetic, but it is decidedly my opinion. I don't think you know half of what goes on here."

"Such as what?"

Her eyes clouded. "Did you know Tanya Rolfe is dying?"

The words caught him like a fist in the stomach. "How do

you know?" But he was remembering how frail she'd looked that morning, remembering the sound of her breath slipping from her lungs.

"I had to rewrite her obituary."

The word puzzled him.

"Her death notice. It's an old custom in journalism—the writers still observe it here. When someone is important, we keep an obituary in the communicator in case they die suddenly. Hers was out of date. Her new conserere had to be added to it, and several sonatas.

"They told me to do it right away. Anyway, you know how I can't seem to keep from meddling . . ." She looked up at him. "One question seemed to bring up another, so I coded the communicator for her medical file."

"Is that why you decided to—eat blackberries forever?"

She shook her head. "Not really." She reached her hand up to him. "Help me up. Walk me back to my cabin and I'll show you."

He reached out a hand to her and pulled her to her feet. They walked down the curving path, not talking, not feeling the need to talk, until they came to the old footbridge that led to Liss's cabin.

"We didn't get any blackberries, did we?" she said at last, looking at the empty basket.

"You'll have a long time for that."

"Will you?"

He pushed open the door to the cabin, striding ahead of her. "I don't know."

She walked to the tall desk and rummaged through a stack of papers, drawing one out. "Read this."

"Your letter to yourself?"

She shook her head. "A poem."

He read, thrumming the cadences with fingers tapping against his knee.

"What do you think?" she asked when he finished. "Be honest."

"I'm always honest," he said.

"I know you are. That's why I wanted you to read it."

"But I'm not a poet."

She sank into a chair next to him and stared at the wide planked floor.

He looked at her for a moment, then he said, "It seems to be quite good. Technically, you've done well and your imagery is—"

"Pedestrian."

"I didn't say that."

"You didn't need to. I can see it in your face."

"I told you I'm not a poet."

"Neither am I." She took the paper from him and folded it in half, creasing the edges with a thumbnail. "I'm a little slow. It took me a long time to find out. But, now that I know, there's no point in drawing it out, is there?"

He considered his words carefully. Then he said, "You have to give yourself time, Liss. We all do. It doesn't come all at once."

"I *have* decided to give myself time. All the time in the world."

"Are you sure?"

"I've thought about it a lot. I'm glib. I'm clever. I have a knack with words. That doesn't make me a poet, David. Not even a fledgling poet. It just isn't there. If I could live forever and not lose whatever creative drive I have—it still wouldn't be enough. I could write until this cabin fell away to dust"— she swept her arm toward the window—"until these mountains crumbled. And it wouldn't matter." Her face twisted. "It's not easy to finally admit to yourself what should have been obvious."

He pulled her to him awkwardly, cradling her head against his shoulder. "What are you going to do now?"

After a few minutes, she sat up. "I have nearly a month to go before my Final Decision, but that won't change anything." She looked at him sharply. "I can still write, you know. Derivative stuff, non-fiction, so on. I suppose I'll do that. I'm basically a compiler anyway. I'm good at it. Not many people are."

She stood up, smoothing her clothes. Then she walked to the tiny dispenser, punched a lever, and extracted two containers of juice. "In a way, it's a relief. I don't have to prove myself anymore." She handed him one and drank deeply from the other. "I don't have to do anything, except be."

He fingered the juice container, wondering what to say to her, saying nothing.

She sat down beside him. "It's funny the way things work out, isn't it?" Her face moved in a wispy little smile. "I never thought it would turn out that I'd be the technician."

Liss ate with a good appetite, while David rearranged his food, absently pushing it into ridges and furrows, eating none.

She chided him. "You're as thin as a spar, now. If you fall away any more, the ants will carry you off."

His face quirked into a smile, but he couldn't eat.

After dinner as the evening sun slipped away in purple shadows, they walked to the open concert hall cantilevered over the lake shore.

"Have you heard any of it yet?" she asked.

He shook his head. "She wouldn't let me see the score." He was going to hear Tanya Rolfe's "Summer Conserere" for the first time that night, and he was acutely aware that it was to be her last work.

They took seats near the rear. Beyond the stage, the last colors of evening blazed pink above the mountains at the far edge of the lake.

"That was planned, you know," said Liss admiring the sunset. "The visiographer is Lindner. I think he's a genius. Nobody else can combine nature and artifice the way he can."

The stage rose silently before them, bearing the conductor and the small orchestra. A hush—then a measured chorus of cicadas began, answered by the flickering lights of a hundred fireflies.

The chorus increased tenfold, as the tiny fireflies became ten thousand points of light wheeling slowly across the darkening sky in constellations of cold fire.

A symphosizer sighed once, then a chorus of wind whispering through new leaves became a theme uttered by a single soloboe.

David felt himself swept away by the music and the subtle changing effects in the sky around him. In turn, he felt love, then grief and a heavy sense of loss, then hope. A throbbing of strings and colors began, so delicate he felt it as pain in the tightness of his throat. Then silence. Black. Night, until a single point of light—a shooting star—grew to a great ball of fire and a swelling chorus of exultation.

He felt tears rise in his eyes and blinked to keep them back. He felt vaguely ashamed of them, and yet they were echoed by bright eyes everywhere in the audience. He joined with the others in applause, rubbing his hands together slowly at first, then more briskly. The leathery rustle of appreciation grew in speed and then the ultimate compliment—spontaneously, the audience began the rhythmic, sighing breathing that symbolized an inspired performance, that symbolized the breath of life.

A single light focused on the slight figure of Tanya Rolfe. She came onto the stage on the arm of Lindner, the visiographer, walking slowly with a halting step. She stood with her head flung back as if to take in more air.

The rhythmic breathing increased in tempo until David's fingers tingled and he felt quite giddy. Next to him, Liss sighed, fluttering on the edge of consciousness. Here and there, people in the audience toppled, overcome by the hyperventilation. And still it went on, until Tanya Rolfe signaled to Lindner and the two walked slowly off the stage.

He left Liss at the path near her cabin.

"You want to be alone?"

He nodded.

"I understand." She kissed him lightly and turned away, then stopped, saying, "David, we've been friends. That's important, isn't it?" She looked at him once again. "Will you tell a friend—when you decide?"

He kissed her then. They clung together like two lost things for a minute or two, and then she gently pushed him away and, without saying goodbye, walked away toward the little footbridge.

He wandered alone for a while, not noticing where he was going until he found himself near Tanya Rolfe's cabin. A light still shone through the window.

He tapped lightly on the door, got no answer, tapped again. The door was unlocked, and he pushed it open.

Still dressed, she lay on the bed. Her eyes were closed. For a shattering moment, he thought she was dead. Then a thin whistling breath escaped from her lungs.

He stood watching her, wanting to wake her, not wanting to. She was like a candle, nearly spent, guttering out with a final glow—defying the night.

He stood for a long time, looking at the tracks of time on her face and body. The tears he had kept back at the concert rolled down his face. "Was it worth it?" he whispered. "Was it worth it?"

He left her cabin, shutting the door softly behind him. He had until tomorrow morning, then Final Decision. Final. No turning back. No changing his mind from that point on.

He walked in the dark for an hour or two, trying to gather himself into one piece and failing. Moonlight glittered on the black lake, and the trees cast shadows of ink. He felt tired and a little disoriented. There was a place up ahead where he could rest.

The path curved to the tiny wood building they called the chapel. He pushed the door open and went in. He had never bothered with it before, but he knew that some of the others had.

He sat back in the dim room and looked down on a small dark arena. The bench he sat on was made of wood with a hard, curving back. In front of him lay a bank of controls. He pressed one at random.

The arena took on a pale blue cast and a three-dimensional hexagram formed. A soft, almost subliminal voice said, "The Star of David." A man with a long white flowing beard clutched two stone tablets. David watched awhile, not really listening as the voice purred on, ". . . Thou shalt not kill."

Thou shalt not kill.

If he stayed, wasn't that what he'd be doing? To himself? A shiver rippled down his back. He pressed the controls.

A circle moved before him—yin and yang—as divided as his mind.

Another button. A cross—with a man pinioned to it. Helpless as a butterfly on a board. Suffering eyes.

Another button. A sunflower, yellow petals opening.

Another. A serpent coiled itself into a figure eight.

Confused, he pressed his hand over the controls to shut it off, but instead, he disengaged the speed. Below him, the scenes changed like shifting crystals in a kaleidoscope. The sunflower melting into a crescent with a star . . . the star flowing into the hexagram . . . unfolding into a cross . . . melting serpent gliding across the face of a yellow flower. All the while, soft voices whispering, ". . . Allah . . . illusion . . . shalt not kill. . . ."

He ran. He ran until the cool night air swept away the shifting scenes in his head.

Back in his cabin with no hope of sleep, he dialed a communicator code. Prints began to tumble out of the machine —a dozen, two dozen, more. . . . The complete works of Tanya Rolfe.

He tuned his cythar and began to play what he could of her music. Sitting cross-legged on the floor, he played, his fingers moving from one set of strings to the other, leaping the ninety-degree angle easily.

Only as he played did his mind relax. No thoughts flickered consciously, but the undercurrent sang from the plucked strings. She wouldn't die, she couldn't die, as long as her music played.

She wouldn't die, she couldn't die. Only when he stopped did he think of his own body falling away in sagging ripples of flesh, falling away to nothing. Only when he stopped did he think of his music and how it would die while he lived on in smooth-muscled emptiness.

He played until his fingers bled, and then he set aside his cythar and fitted his flute together.

He fingered through the copies of her music, leaving little smears of blood on the pages. Then he came to the title-page of her last conserere.

He read:

SUMMER CONSERERE
by
Tanya Rolfe

And below that, the dedication:

To David Defour, who lives on.

Why hadn't she told him? Why hadn't she? He felt a lump grow in his throat that was too hard and dry for tears.

He looked at the inscription knowing that the meaning could be taken two ways, knowing also that it could have had only one meaning to Tanya Rolfe. And he knew, too, why she hadn't told him.

She knew he had to decide for himself.

When the night faded to shades of gray, he left the cabin carrying only a thin set of panpipes and a small recording device slung on his belt.

Exhaustion had brought its own kind of peace. Spent, he sank down at the foot of a wide beech tree near the clearing. The first glow of the new sun began to color the hills.

He crushed a blade of grass with his sore fingers, rolling it between them, inhaling its sharp, sweet smell.

It was good to be alive. What would it be like to not be? To not find out what lay beyond the next day? To not see Thursday? To never slide down the hills of April?

A rabbit rustled at the edge of the blackberry patch, nibbled tentatively at a blade of grass, thrust cut-velvet ears in his direction. He felt pity for it. It was so small, so ephemeral. Its moments fleeting as he watched.

But it had to be what it was.

He reached for the panpipes and blew a melody in a minor key to the little creature. It was a theme, he remembered, from Beethoven. He didn't know just why the theme seemed important to him, but somehow it did. Somehow, it told him of the end of things—and of beginnings. The melody hung in the warm sweet air for a moment, and somehow that moment seemed a bit more alive to him.

Then the ideas, the variations, came tumbling out of his

panpipes. He laughed and touched the tiny recorder slung from his hip. And in his mind he could hear the orchestration —swelling strings, then the theme whispered from a flute, answered by a kleidelphone, echoed by the dark double reeds. Now a muttered tympani, a variation by Weidner horn. It was all there. It was all there because it was his lot to create.

And he realized suddenly that he was outrageously hungry. No wonder. It was getting late. It was time for him to tell them he was going to stay at Renascence—but only if they'd give him breakfast.

Chapter 7

Liss had said to him once, "You don't need people, David."

He had taken that thought and turned it over in his mind and accepted it.

It was a lie. He knew that now.

David began to shake. He tried to control it, but as he tried, the trembling grew worse until it seemed as if his body were trying to fly apart, trying to separate itself from its core of hurt. With a hand that barely obeyed, he threw open the cabin door and rushed out into the dimming light.

The mountain wilderness pressed in around him, making him feel vulnerable and utterly alone. It had been a long time since he'd felt that way about Renascence—not since his first days there when the memories of Vesta were fresh.

He looked up in the darkening sky. A satellite skimmed faintly overhead. And there, another. For a minute his thoughts shot out of him, projecting him into the sky, far beyond the satellites to the asteroid he'd once called home. Back to the little boy he'd been in a Vesta dormitory. But it wasn't any use. That little boy was gone. Dead. Finished.

It was nearly dark. Flicking on the little light he carried on his belt, he walked on along the familiar paths through dark woods. He came to a clearing and began to cut across the grassy meadow. Something moved once in the shadows and was gone.

He found the fawn near the soft clay banks of a spring

run. A bobcat had killed it. The cat's prints lay deep in the beam of his light. A hemlock branch above the kill bent from the recent weight it had supported. The cat had waited, watching the fawn in the grass at the edge of the clearing. Then it had leaped, landing on the little deer's spine, paralyzing it with sharp claws.

The fawn lay warm beside him, its guts spilling in an obscene heap by his feet. He ran his hand over its head, its ears. He whispered, "Does everything have to die at Renascence?" Blind eyes stared back. Anguish tore at his soul and left it as ruined as the young deer. It was the same fawn he was sure. The one he'd seen at dawn three weeks ago.

Leaving it, he stumbled away toward the spot where he'd waited alone that morning. He felt a grim satisfaction that the bobcat would go hungry while he was there. It wouldn't dare come back to its meal while a human was around.

He lowered himself to the damp ground, cradling his head in his cupped hands, looking at nothing as the moon rose over the back of the mountain. The ring he wore pressed into his scalp. He raised his hand to his face, trying to see the ring in the dim light. Abruptly, he tugged at it, meaning to pull it off, fling it away, as if the action would undo that morning three weeks ago when they'd put it on his finger.

It was too tight. He would wear it always. He turned his face to the ground as great racking sobs shuddered through him.

He'd felt lightheaded and a little shaky when he'd stood up in the early light three weeks ago. He had narrowed his eyes against the rising sun that reddened the sky over Trey Mountain. The small wooden buildings of Renascence lay in the deep shadow of the hills.

He was hungry. He hadn't eaten for nearly two days.

He wiped the dew from his panpipes onto the rough cloth of his outer shirt and hooked the little instrument to his belt. Across the clearing, a fawn browsing at the new grass on the forest's edge froze at his movement.

He froze too, looking at it, thinking, it's all right. All right, pretty thing. No one here wants to hurt you.

They stood for a full minute looking at each other. Then it moved and was gone in the rising mists of a spring that ran from among the roots of a dark hemlock.

He made his way toward one of the buildings, feeling the grass give beneath his feet. The dining hall was empty. He was glad for that; he wasn't ready just yet to talk to anyone. The communicator screen showed him the breakfast choices and he punched up the code for two complete meals. Piling all the food on one tray, he carried it outside to the edge of the lake and walked across the narrow stone bridge to a tiny island near the shore. He sat down leaning his back against a tree, balancing his tray across his knees.

He poured great gouts of honey and cream over the bowl of hot oatmeal. Eating too fast for tasting, he tried not to let the thoughts that lay just beneath his mind bubble to the surface; he allowed himself only one—eat now.

The mist rose like a thousand smokes from the lake. He pushed his food aside and raised a steaming cup to his lips. In an hour—in less than an hour—Final Decision.

The food lay heavy on his stomach.

He would sit there for the hour, he would tell them what he'd decided, and then maybe he could sleep.

He crumbled a crust of bread between his fingers, mounding it in a heap. Bit by bit, he tossed it into the water. Bream rose to feed. Their hungry mouths sent small ripples through the water. David watched the widening circles as if he were hypnotized until a splash sent its wake toward the little island.

It was M'Kumbe. The tall black boy walked naked through the shallows toward a deeper part of the lake. Soon he was swimming, long thin arms pulling his body through the cold water. Early sunlight glinted on his wet skin.

The boy swam on, passing close to David's island, not looking, not speaking. It was a matter of privacy for them both. Both made Final Decision that morning.

Across the lake in the dark trees, a wood thrush sang a song of melting sadness.

When the hour was up, David walked the short way back to the dining hall and left off his tray. A group of twelve-year-olds pushed past him in chattering confusion. They made him feel old—older than sixteen. Without speaking, he walked the path along the lake toward the open pavilion.

People were waiting for him. There were three of them wearing mole-gray robes brightened with the hoods of their art. Rose pink, for music, fell from the robe of one—Tanya Rolfe. She had been his teacher for five years, he thought, and he had seen her nearly every day. But, how different she looked in her robe. So frail. So old now. Delicate as the moth he'd found in his cabin. It bore rose spots on its soft gray wings. He'd saved it in a little box for a long time, and then he'd opened it one day, and as he touched the small creature, it fell away to dust.

He looked at the others. A tall man with a gray-black beard showed the gold of science. The last, a dark-eyed woman, wore the white of arts and letters. The three sat together on a wide platform facing the lake.

A wind rose from across the water, ruffling his hair, stirring the soft robes of the three. No one spoke. In a minute, M'Kumbe came and stood beside him, and then a girl called Sabra. Dry tear-tracks stained her face.

Tanya Rolfe spoke first in a voice as thin and old as cracking parchment. "Once before, you three stood before a committee much like this one. You pledged your changing years to test yourselves. Now, you have come to Final Decision." She paused to draw a shallow breath through failing lungs. "Today, you must choose your path. There is no turning back." She looked away then, across the lake as if across a great distance.

The tall man began to read from a thin roll of paper:

"When death died, when humankind held immortality in its grasp, it exulted. Now was time rolled out forever. Time to contemplate. To sow. To reap.

"But, immortality brought another death—the death of creativity, the stilling of that drive in humankind to reach beyond itself into forever.

"And so, humankind had to designate its special children as guardians of the arts. It had to say to them, 'Be mortal, some of you, so that all our lives may have meaning.'

"You are these children, these guardians." He paused and

then he said, "You have come to the day of Final Decision. And so I put the question to you—do you choose physical immortality with the full knowledge that it will bring the death of your art? Or do you deny, knowing that your only immortality will be that of such creative works as live after you?"

The man looked at them, then said, "How do you choose, M'Kumbe Elthree?"

The black boy touched long fingers together, lightly, yet with the tension of steel springs. "I choose—I choose to deny—"

"I will read the Charge of Mortality," said the man. "At that point you must confirm."

David's head seemed to hum. The man's voice ran together in meaningless sounds. And then he heard M'Kumbe say, "I confirm."

"And you, Sabra Beseven? How do you choose?"

The girl's voice rose in a shaky soprano, "I choose immortality."

"I will read the Charge of Immortality. After which you must confirm."

The girl nodded. Tears began to course down her face.

The man read from the thin paper again. "With the choice of immortality, you, Sabra Beseven, confirm that the application of your art, that of creative thought in the field of science, will no longer be your work. You confirm that any further work in this field will necessarily be confined to the work of technician. You further confirm that the right to reproduce yourself is denied by law and by the immortality process itself unless specifically countermanded by the Ministry of Population. Do you so confirm?"

"I do."

The man's eyes fell on David. "How do you choose, David Defour?"

He felt giddy, as if he were going to lose his balance. After a few seconds he said, "I choose to deny."

The man nodded almost imperceptibly. "I will read the Charge of Mortality. At that point you must confirm:

"With the choice of mortality, you, David Defour, confirm that physical death is a certainty. You confirm that the choice of mortality is no guarantee of the success of your art, that of music and composition. You further confirm the right to marry and reproduce yourself if you so choose."

His throat felt dry. He tried to say the final words and with an effort they came out. "I—confirm." His head whirled.

The next few minutes blurred forever in his mind. At one point, he knew he reached toward the girl next to him and tried to say, "No. Please don't cry," but he had no air, it seemed, to thrust the words out. At another point, he saw the tear-bright eyes of Tanya Rolfe shining from her wrinkled face. Someone took his hand and pressed a ring on his finger. He looked at it. And then, through a trick of light perhaps, a flash from the brilliant sun onto the gold and black of the ring blazed the design into his brain forever—a broken symbol of infinity—and then the words: "For Art."

He left the pavilion and walked through the woods back to his cabin. He pushed open the door. The room was a confusion of paper, heaps of paper—the complete works of Tanya Rolfe. He had dialed them the night before and the communicator had spit them into his room. The scores lay everywhere: on the floor, propped on his music stand, layered in fanning sheets across the communicator bank and the symphosizer keyboard that stood against one wall.

One sheet lay on top. It was the title page of Tanya Rolfe's new conserere, and underneath her name, the dedication:

To David Defour, who lives on.

He was exhausted; he hadn't slept. He'd played her music through the night.

Pushing the lever for his bed, he threw himself on it when it unrolled.

When he closed his eyes, all he could see was a shining gold ring and a broken lazy figure eight. After a time, he slept.

Moth wings brushed across his lips.
He stirred.
Moth wings brushed his eyes. "Poor David."

"What—" He opened his eyes and looked up. Frank blue eyes stared back. "Oh, Liss," he said, "what time is it?"

"Time you got up. It's nearly supper." She waggled a basket under his nose. "I've brought us a picnic."

His legs and arms felt heavy—as if he'd been drugged. He rubbed his eyes and then, at the touch of cool metal, pulled his hand away and stared stupidly at the ring he wore.

The girl took his hand in hers and looked at the ring for a few moments, then she stood up. "Come on. Let's eat. You're much too thin to miss meals." She reached for his hand and tugged. Protesting, he let himself be led outside.

They walked in silence for a while past the cabins toward the lake. When Liss didn't turn off toward the island, he said, "Where are we going?"

"Someplace different."

They walked along the edge of the lake and stood on the grassy earthen dam. In the center, the water plunged over a spillway. Nothing but forest lay below them.

"Uncharted territory, so to speak." Liss had begun to climb down the steep side of the spillway. In a moment, all he could see was the top of her head.

He stood watching her as her head poked up over the rocks. "Well, come on."

"Come on, where?"

"To the bottom."

He walked to the edge and looked over. The spillway ended and the remains of a natural waterfall course fell on beyond it. It was steep. He hesitated.

Liss looked up. "Come on. If I can do it lugging this basket, you can do it empty handed."

Still sleepy, he shook his head in puzzlement and swung a leg down onto the rocks below. Reaching for handholds, he clambered down. Spray from the spillway misted over him. Here and there, moss grew on the rocks, turning to slick jelly under the pressure of his fingers.

When he reached the bottom, he looked up. He couldn't see the man-made spillway from there, only the water roaring over polished rocks. They were in a narrow gorge. Steep-sided hills rose on either side. At points, the tree branches met overhead sending broken sunlight through their leaves to dance on the water below.

Liss had moved on, making a path—here walking on fairly level ground; there grabbing a branch to keep from falling into the foaming pool at the foot of the waterfall. They came to a series of flat rocks. Stepping from one to another, she crossed. Water poured between the rocks as the stream continued its downward plunge. She stopped on a wide rock ledge and set down the basket.

He followed. She sat on the rock, pulled off her shoes, and plunged her feet into the frigid pool.

"How did you find this place?" he asked.

She wiggled her toes in the water. "Most people here go up on the mountain to think. I come down here. Take off your shoes and dunk your toes. It's good for your brain."

"I can imagine," he said wryly.

"It is. Cools off fevered thoughts and brows."

"Well, in that case, I guess I'd better." He pulled off his shoes, laying them next to hers, and thrust his feet into the water. Across the pool the water poured in a steady cascade, spreading its mist in a cloud through walls of green trees. Along one side, a thicket of pink mountain laurel bloomed.

"I think it's symbolic," she said.

"What is?"

"This place. It's at the edge."

"The edge?"

"The edge of Renascence. We're at the boundary here." She pointed toward the waterfall, "Up there is what we've known. It's safe and civilized. But all around us is wilderness —the unknown, like our future."

He considered this. He said nothing.

"I guess you're not used to symbolic thinking, though. Are you, technician?"

He laughed. It had been a long time since he'd resented her calling him that, not since they'd first come to Renascence, not since they were a couple of scared eleven-year-olds. "Not everybody from Vesta is a technician," he said.

She looked at the ring he wore, then looked away, and as

she looked away the rising mist from the waterfall seemed to enter her eyes. "No. I guess not everybody."

He lay back across the rock, cradled his head in his cupped hands and looked up at the sky. "Do you ever miss living up there in the Belt, Liss? Do you miss it at all?"

She leaned back, cushioning her head on his shoulder. "I did for a while. I still do—some. But I'll miss Earth worse. I know I will."

He felt his voice grow stilted as he said, "You're still going then? You're sure about your Final Decision?"

"I'm sure."

"You won't miss not having a child?"

"I don't know. I've never had one and I don't miss it now. Since so few immortals are allowed to have one, I guess it won't matter. I'll just keep on taking after-pills," she said, "and go on like before." She looked up, squinting against the blue sky. "The hardest thing is the way I feel about my parents. I'm afraid they'll be disappointed. You never knew yours, David, so maybe you don't know what I mean, but mine are mortal—everything they live for is their art. My mother's poetry, my father's painting—these things mean everything to them. But, I can't live up to them. I'm a poet without virtue."

"What do you mean?"

"Didn't you ever read Aristotle?" She peeped at him slyly, little laugh lines forming at the corners of her eyes.

He scowled, trying to look stern.

She laughed, "Oh, you *are* still a technician—"

"Well, you can't make an L-5 out of an Echo."

She rolled over and looked down at him, wrinkling up her little nose sprinkled with brown-sugar freckles. "Anyway, Aristotle said, 'The virtue of a knife is to cut.' So, it follows that the virtue of a poet is to produce poetry." She looked away for a moment, serious now. "If what I produce isn't poetry, then that makes me a poet without virtue. That's why I'm leaving, David."

He didn't answer; he was looking at her nose. It seemed to him that it was the most delicious-looking nose in all creation. He reached up and took gentle hold of her ears, pulled her down to him and then he kissed that nose and the lips underneath. Somehow, he couldn't stop. His hand slid down her throat and rested on her breast.

They had made love before, casually, or out of a strong physical need, or even to comfort one another, but it was different now. She was leaving in a few weeks; he was staying. Somehow that made it more precious—almost unbearably precious. "Oh, Liss," he whispered.

Their clothes commingled in an untidy heap and cushioned their yielding bodies against the hard flat rock.

He loved her. For the first time he knew it—knew that she knew it, too. He loved her, and it echoed in the throbbing of his body and the pounding of his heart. She couldn't go. She couldn't. If she did, what would become of him?

He shuddered and clung to her.

After a time, they drew apart, and when they did it was more than a simple separation. It was as if the chill of space intervened and drew her away from him, pulling her back to the colony she was born to. "You're really going?" he said finally.

"Yes."

They pulled on their clothes silently. Then they spread out their food and picked at it with the pretense of appetite. The sky grew red with sunset. In the thick brush a wood thrush penetrated the rush of waterfall with a song so sweet, so sad that David felt his heart constrict.

Her hands moved, putting things away in the little basket, packing. "We'd better go," she said, "it's getting late."

When he came back, his cabin was clean, his bed rolled, and the untidy piles of music had been stacked neatly. He was puzzled. Up to now the cleaning, or the lack of it, had been left largely to him.

The red message light glowed on the communicator. He pressed it. A voice said, "The mortal colonies of Earth, its satellites, and the neighboring asteroids welcome you, David Defour, to their society.

"Certain privileges come with your decision for mortal life. You now have at your disposal quite a large allowance for

goods and services. And, in two years when you join the Society of Adults, unlimited travel allowances will also be yours.

"Do you have any requests at this time?"

He thought about it. He could get something for Liss. To
keep. A necklace maybe. Something she could see and touch
that would remind her of him. Something—the thought lay
just below the surface—something that might change her
mind about leaving. It needed to be symbolic; she loved symbols.

He couldn't think of anything.

Then, it came to him. He could give her one of those
purple stones they found at Renascence now and then. What
were they? Amethyst.

He punched the vocorder. "I'd like a necklace. For a girl."

"Certainly. Details, please."

"An amethyst. Set in gold. On a chain."

"Do you have any further requests?"

He stood pondering the question. He'd had everything he
needed, really. There wasn't anything else except—His eyes
fell on his cythar. It leaned up against the music stand in the
center of the room. He'd had it for years; he'd brought it with
him from Vesta. It was a good one, with a rich deep tone, and
yet. . . .

He pressed the vocorder and said, "May I have a new
cythar?"

"Certainly. Details, please."

A new cythar—any kind he wanted. "Handmade with
realgut strings." He paused, thinking about it. He could have
any kind he wanted—the best. Hesitantly, he said, "One made
by Schimmermann, please. A good one."

"Received. Place your hand over the visio so that the ring
you wear imprints."

He raised his hand. The metal of the ring caused a momentary blue glow to flash on the screen.

"Received."

He sat down and contemplated his good fortune. A
Schimmermann. He was going to own a real Schimmermann
cythar. He looked at his old one. He'd learned to play on it.
He picked it up and turned it over in his hands. The body of

the instrument was scarred a little from years of use. He ran his fingers over the strings, plucking softly. His flute and his cythar were the only things he had left from his old life on Vesta. That, and his name, Defour—D-4, the number of the crib they'd placed him in when he was born. He looked at the cythar, feeling as if he'd been disloyal to it. He didn't want to give it up. He put it down, went back to the communicator, and pushed the vocorder again. "My old cythar," he said, "may I keep it? May I have them both?"

"Certainly."

He grinned. And then his sudden affluence went to his head. He said, "And I want some ice cream. Now. All different kinds with chocolate syrup on top." He started to place his ring against the visio and then he paused as invention came to him. "And on top of that, I want a banana all cut up. And then a peach. And then more chocolate."

Tanya Rolfe smiled at him, and the smile increased the wrinkles on her face in geometric proportions. "I see you have a new cythar."

He nodded. He sat in a chair in her cabin, holding the instrument to him. It was everything he'd hoped for, and more.

"And did you order everything you could think of, David, with your newfound wealth?"

"Well, this," he ran his fingers over the smooth body of the instrument. "And a necklace for Liss." Then, with a sheepish look, "and a tub of ice cream."

She laughed. "I remember what I did. I didn't practice my music for nearly a week. My little room was brimming over with things until there wasn't any room for *me*. And then do you know what I did?"

He shook his head.

"I sent nearly everything back, and I gave most of the rest away." She looked at him keenly. "When we know we can have nearly everything we want—at any time, then the need seems to vanish and we don't really want it anymore. At least that's the way it works for so many of us. But—" She brushed her hands together, dismissing the problem. "We're wasting your lesson. Let me see what you've been doing with your variation from Beethoven."

Resting his cythar against his chair, he pressed a code on the communicator. Sheets bearing his latest composition rolled out of the machine.

She looked them over, holding them close to her failing eyes. Then she said, "Good, David. Good."

He couldn't believe it. No corrections? No changes? He waited cautiously, sure that she had more to say.

Finally, she took his firm hands in hers. "It's the best you've done."

He flushed with pleasure. It was the first undiluted praise she'd ever given him. He didn't know what to say.

She leaned back in her chair, her breath coming in reedy little gasps. She looked at him for a moment through half-closed eyes and then she said, "I wonder now, David, where you're going with this?"

His elation collapsed. There just wasn't any pleasing her in the final analysis. None at all. "I thought you liked it."

"I do."

"Then what is it?" He clutched the score, rumpling it between his fingers. "Is it the ending? Do you think it's too short? You think it's incomplete—"

"Oh, David." The smile again. "David, David. You don't listen. I will tell you again. It's the best thing you've done. Now, where are you going with this?"

"I don't know what you mean."

She didn't speak for a moment. Then she said, "Go to the window there and look out."

His eyebrow quirked. She was getting old. Humoring her, he got up and walked to the window of her cabin.

"What do you see?"

"Woods. A creek. Then a green field on the other side."

"What else?"

He didn't know what she was talking about, but he said, "Not much else. Just the trees. The creek and a bridge. Then, the field."

"And where are you, David?"

He found this line of talk exasperating. Obviously, she

didn't mean for him to say he was standing by the window. She liked to talk in riddles and symbols—just like Liss. They were a pair. When they did this to him, he felt annoyed and a little backward, as if he were a dim child who couldn't quite comprehend. He felt his lips press together.

She asked him again, "Where are you now?"

He knew she'd keep pecking away at him until he got her point. He looked out of the window again. Tall oaks, heavy with green, towered over the cabin. The understory thinned near the creek. A small stone footbridge led across. He shook his head.

"And where was Beethoven," she prompted.

He didn't know what she meant, and then suddenly it came to him. Beethoven was a transitional composer, leading the way from the old Classical period to the Romantic. "Beethoven was on the bridge," he said.

She laughed softly, "Good. Now, come sit down, David. I won't torture you with any more symbols."

He sat down and faced her. He felt a smile play around his lips. "You're trying to tell me something so that I won't forget."

"It helps our focus sometimes to do that," she said. "You're on the bridge, too, David. I want you to think about where it is you're going."

"You mean, my music's transitional."

She nodded. "Can you see where it's going?"

It was going to the only place it could, he thought. He had no idea how to answer her. His music just was. And if it were going someplace, it seemed that it had aimed itself there without help from him.

She sat waiting for him to answer.

What did she want of him, anyway? It made him uneasy, this analyzing she put him through. He searched for an answer that would satisfy her. "Well," he said finally, "we're in the Tertiary Romantic period now, but—"

"But?" Her eyes searched his.

"Well, it leaves something out, don't you think?" She didn't speak, making him feel as if he had to go on. "I mean, the emotions in the music. . . . They're beautiful. The mu-

sic's beautiful, but everything isn't always beautiful. It's so
high-flown. It just isn't real."

"You mean, it doesn't reflect life?"

He thought about that for a moment, then he nodded.
"Yes. I guess that's it."

"So that's where you're going, David. Into a new real-
ism."

His dark eyes widened slightly; he'd never thought of that
before.

Her voice was soft. "It would be an interesting path." She
looked out of the cabin window, but she seemed not to see.
After a few moments, she said to him, "And how will you
make your music real, David?"

"I'm not sure, yet," he said, "but I know there's a way.
Part of it is in multi-modal work, the way you work with a
visiographer. But it's more than holos moving in and out of
music." His dark eyes glowed as he talked, "It's more than
that. I feel it. More than pretty sunsets blending with soloboes
and fireflies—" He stopped, blushing furiously. He was hid-
eously embarrassed; he'd been talking, without realizing it,
about Tanya Rolfe's latest work—her "Summer Conserere."
He blurted, "I'm sorry. I didn't mean that."

Surprisingly, she laughed. "Of course you meant it,
David." She reached out and patted his hand. "You had no
choice. You have your own music. Don't apologize for that.
You have to send your music out of your soul like a monu-
ment. Like the song these mountains sing here at Renascence."

His eyes grew wide and questioning.

She patted his hand again. She nodded. "Oh, yes. These
mountains sing, David. The birds know it."

If Liss had knocked at his door, he hadn't heard it. He sat
on the floor and twiddled dials and pushed buttons on an array
of miniaturized equipment littering the floor. Stacks of communicator print-outs teetered precariously on his desk while a
stray sheet or two rose and fell in the breeze from his window.
He was totally absorbed in what he was doing.

She stood for a full minute in the doorway watching him,

then she said, "No wonder you're so thin. Your eat-meter is broken."

He looked up. "Hello, Liss."

"I thought you'd call me for supper, but I can see now you never got a single hunger pang."

He grinned. "What would I do without you to look after me?"

She looked at him thoughtfully. "I guess you'll have to learn."

He didn't seem to hear her. His head bent low over the litter on the floor. He seemed to be listening to something else.

"Maybe I'd better put you up for adoption," she said softly.

"What?"

"Nothing. What are you doing?"

"Working on a new piece. Tanya gave me the idea. Want to hear some of it?"

"You mean you're actually going to let me hear one of your compositions before it's finished?"

"This one time." His hands flew, adjusting dials, touching here and there. "It's not a composition. It's a fragment. A component." He touched a last dial, touched again, said, "There."

She waited for the music to begin. Nothing happened. Nothing at all. "What—" she began.

He put his fingers to his lips. "Wait."

She waited. The room was silent. Then she began to giggle. "David, you're brilliant. A real innovator. Music without sound. You've given me an idea for a poem." She rummaged at his music stand and found a piece of staved paper. Turning it over to its blank back side, she pretended to write. "There." She handed it to him. "My masterpiece."

He held the sheet in his hand, not looking at it at all, but staring at her in a most intent way.

"David?" She tilted her head at him and shook it in mock sorrow. She made little "*tch-tch*" sounds with her tongue. Then she said, "I remember when you were a whole and somewhat sound individual. Poor David. It's tragic what starvation can do." She reached for his hand. "Let's go eat, while we can. It's going to rain."

A delighted grin spread over his face. "No, it's not."

She let go of his hand and stared at him.

"It's not going to rain." He grinned again—wider. "Look." He showed her one of the dials. A green line pulsed up and down leaving a faint luminous trail behind it.

"That's music?"

"Not yet. But, that's your rain—and that." He pushed a small box toward her.

Her nose wrinkled slightly. Liss glanced out of the window, puzzled. "David, what are you talking about?"

"This." He pointed at the dial again. "Remember the storm yesterday?"

She nodded.

"I recorded it."

She raised an eyebrow slightly. "I don't hear any thunder."

"There isn't any," he said. "It's the sound of the storm itself—the air disturbances, changes in ionization. The storm was miles away when I recorded it. And the sound was below the audible range—infrasound."

"But, I don't hear anything."

"Of course not. You can't. It's too low to hear. But it's not too low to feel. You're not aware of it though. It's subliminal." He sat on the floor, holding his knees, looking up at her with an air of supreme satisfaction.

"What does the box have to do with it?"

"Oh. Ions. It's an ionizer. I just used it to simulate unstable storm conditions. I set it to fluctuate from positive to negative."

"So, I have been effectively deceived." Liss plopped to the floor next to him, sitting cross-legged amid the litter. "Tell me, technician, is this Art?"

His grin faded, "Don't you see the possibilities?"

"Not really. Unless you want to empty your outdoor concert halls. Who wants to sit in the rain?"

"It's what you do all the time, Liss, in your poetry. It's symbolic."

"Infrasound metaphors?"

"Yes." He seemed delighted that she understood. "With infrasound, I can transplant people with music."

"With thunderstorms?" The eyebrow quirked again.

"I'm trying to tell you," he said with a touch of irritation. "If I write music about Renascence, people will feel it. They'll feel the weather, the mountains—"

"The mountains?"

"That's right. They give off infrasound too, Liss. Through tectonic movements. The birds know it. That's one of the ways they navigate during migration. Every mountain range has a different sound, a different feel—" A look came across his face; it was as if he were hearing something far away, seeing something beyond sight. "They're beacons, Liss. The mountains are beacons."

They finished their supper, stacked their trays and stepped outside the dining hall. They walked the path together, hands touching now and then as if to reaffirm a closeness. "There's a play in the Shed," said Liss. "Want to go?"

He walked for a while without answering, then he said, "No. I don't want to see a play tonight. I want—" He looked at her shyly. "I want to see you. I've got something for you. A present."

She stopped and looked at him. A smile spread over her face, then suddenly, without a ripple it was gone. "It's a going-away present, I guess."

His eyes searched her face, "It doesn't have to be."

She turned away from him and looked out over the lake. Her hands touched together, fingers stroked each other, pulled apart, touched again. "Don't make it so hard, David."

He thrust his hands deep in his pockets, took a step away from her, stopped. They stood facing away from each other. A minute passed, then two, and then they were turning, touching, saying together, "I'm sorry," then laughing at the coincidence.

Their lips brushed in a whisper of a kiss. "Liss—" he began, stopping when he felt his voice begin to break.

Her eyes were blue mist. She shook her head just barely

and touched a stilling finger to his lips. "We have three days, David. That's all. Then they'll send me home."

He drew in a slow breath, found his voice and found that he didn't want to use it. He had wanted to ask if she'd remember him. But it wasn't a fair question. Better to ask if she'd remember the mountains after they crumbled away. Better not to ask at all.

After a few moments, he reached in his pocket again and drew out the little necklace with its single amethyst. He fumbled with the chain, trying to open the tiny catch. Failing, he closed his hand on it, pressing it into a little wad of chain and stone, and put it in her hand.

She didn't look at it; the tears were filling up her eyes too fast for looking. She managed a half-choked "Thank you," then she was running away from him, head down, hand curled tight around the necklace. In a moment, she was gone.

He didn't want to be alone. He most especially didn't want to be alone just then. If he stayed by himself for very long, he knew that a flood of emotion would rise up and drown him. He looked down the path where Liss had run and he wanted to follow, but he couldn't.

The setting sun colored the mountains with purple. He began to walk, cutting away from the path, moving through the woods. Without planning it, he found himself at Tanya Rolfe's cabin.

The door was unlocked. He knocked, received no answer, pushed open the door and stepped inside.

She was sitting in a chair by the window. The glow of the setting sun tinted her thin white hair with rose and pink. A strand of her hair caught in the breeze rose and fell, rose and fell.

Nothing else moved.

Nothing.

He felt a heavy cold begin in his stomach. He felt it spread. "Tanya?" He moved closer to her chair. In the evening light, her skin gave off a faint yellow cast as if it had been coated with the thinnest layer of wax. Her open eyes stared at the dying evening light and gave back none. Her hands lay in her lap, still, fingers lightly curled as if pressed to the keys of a musical instrument. The setting sun reflected on a slim black and gold ring with a broken symbol of eternity.

The cold spread through him, numbing him, freezing him in his footsteps. So this was the way it ended. This was the final thing. The final note dying away until nothing was left, not an echo, nothing.

He'd never seen death before. Never. He'd never even seen age until he'd come to Renascence. He looked at her with mingled fear and love and horror, and the horror of it was that nothing was there at all. There had been music and speech and thought and now there was nothing.

He had to do something. He looked wildly around the room, staring at her things—her music stand, her thin old china teapot, her cup that sat nearly full of cooling tea.

He thought, at last, of the communicator. He ran to it, reached out with hands that shook, and pressed an emergency code.

Finally, the doctor came.

The sobs racked his body and sucked the breath from him until he thought he must be dying. Hot tears ran through his fingers and dripped onto the cold damp earth.

At last, he stretched out face down on the moonlit ground, drained of tears, dry of emotion, conscious only of the scent of earth and crushed grass in his nostrils and a heavy aching fatigue.

At the edge of the meadow the torn body of the little deer cooled rapidly in the mountain night, while nearby, among the black shadows of brush and trees, a hungry bobcat waited.

Chapter 8

Dayglow was beginning to fade when Kurt Kraus debarked from the skiptor. The Vestans in the Arrow boarding area stared curiously at him and at the man who accompanied him, the man with graying hair and hawk eyes—the man who had no legs.

He glided alongside Kurt on the rubberized treads of his prosthesis. They entered the Arrow together. Kurt took the seat reserved for him. The man swung beside. In response to a neural command, the prosthesis lowered him to a sitting position. The Arrow began to move, accelerating rapidly through a tunnel. Then it burst into the open periphery of the asteroid. The artificial sunset glowed on the walls of housing clusters. Clumps of trees cast long shadows over the turf.

As the Arrow sped beyond Dome-Lake Park, Kurt could see City Central in the distance. He looked around him. The Arrow passengers stared back. He could feel hostility mixed with their curiosity. The hostility was growing. It was more open, more evident, on each new trip he made to the colony, and it was directed toward the people of Earth and the mortals of Renascence.

The rift had been widening between Earth and the Belt. Vesta was the epicenter of the discontent, which had spread in broadening circles until it influenced all the colonies, even to the Guardian Force of L-5—the Guardian Force that controlled the warheads of WorldCo from the high ground of

LeGrange, the Guardian Force that had ensured the peace for nearly two hundred years.

With each ripple of dissatisfaction, WorldCo's Ministry had responded, yet in spite of coercion from Commerce and Industry, in spite of the guidance of Education and the subtler, yet pervasive, efforts of Communication, the chasm deepened.

Kurt considered the problem as the Arrow whisked him and his companion to City Central. He looked at the man next to him—the man WorldCo hoped was the key to the solution—Jesus Ramirez, the man who had conceived and developed the Ramirez Star Drive.

The serving dishes glided in a slow ellipse around the table. Kurt took a serving of Vestan duck as it wheeled by him.

The host smiled cherubically as he watched the men and women of the Ministry. And as he watched, he fingered the heavy silver T that hung at his throat.

Thin cylinders, flared at the top, passed by, half-full of a straw-colored liquid. "I hope you'll try our wine," said Silvio. "It's from the Riesling grape. Earth stock, but the minerals in Vestan soil give it a distinctive flavor."

Kurt lifted his glass and sipped appreciatively as he looked at his host. He had not seen him since the day he and the cryptists inspected the children's records at Vesta Central. He remembered their somewhat puzzled report after Mallory questioned the man. "I just can't believe he's lying, Mr. Kraus. Perhaps it really was accidental . . . although I don't quite see how. . . ."

He stared covertly at Tarantino. He seemed quite affable, this little dark-eyed man. He seemed quite open. What was it about him that was disturbing? The man ate little, drank little. His protocol was flawless. He seemed to be the perfect combination of relaxed deference and quick intelligence—exactly right for an Under Minister. Too exact, perhaps. Too perfect. His eyes narrowed slightly as he looked at Tarantino. Something hung at the edges of his memory—something very long ago. But as he tried to grasp it, it slipped away.

When the meal was over, the service sector of the table disappeared into a lower level. It was replaced by flared snifters one-quarter filled with an excellent fortified wine, again Riesling, but syrupy, with a tang to its sweetness.

Heinrich Richter, envoy to Prime Minister Gerstein, opened the meeting. After the formal introductions, he began with carefully worded diplomatic language to explore the relations between Earth and the colonies. This was in prelude to WorldCo's formal proposal. When it came, no one at the table was surprised. Each had been carefully briefed in advance. The meeting was in formal and open deference to the colonies.

"And so," said Richter in his careful voice, "in recognition of a deep, and perhaps archetypal human need, we perceive that when horizons draw near and frontiers close, human beings grow uneasy. When the catalyst of immortal life is added, a future without goals, without aspirations, becomes untenable.

"Until now, even with the knowledge of life everlasting, our horizons have been restricted to the planets and planetoids that circle this little sun. The stars seemed reachable only through centuries of boredom in constricted surroundings—a journey to nowhere, a fool's errand. Now, through the dedication of this man," and here Richter indicated Jesus Ramirez, "our horizons have once again expanded. With the Ramirez Drive, the galaxy can be ours. It is our hope, our intention, to reunite the people of Earth and the colonies in this outreach. Once again, humankind will seek a goal. Once again, humankind will join its mind and its spirit in a quest— a quest for self-fulfillment and knowledge that will lead to the ends of the universe."

To Kurt, the dross of the envoy's rhetoric was consumed by the bright fire at its center. He looked at the man beside him and he felt a fierce pride. He was a product of Renascence, this man, a true immortal in an aging, damaged body. Because of him, because of Renascence, people could begin to dream again.

The formal discussion began and proceeded around the table. Just before Kurt's statement, a man entered the room, spoke briefly to Silvio and then stepped to Kurt's side and handed him a message.

He read it. It was only a few words: "Tanya Rolfe is dead. She died peacefully at Renascence."

He gave his statement automatically. Without conscious thought, his prepared speech rolled out with the accuracy of a computer, while part of him retreated to a hidden place where no one reached, where no one could.

When the meeting broke up into informal groups, he excused himself and left abruptly.

By the time Kurt had accepted the fact that his plan to get thoroughly drunk had failed, it was very late. He left his hotel room and began to walk the streets of Vesta. He avoided the zont and the main publicway and stuck to the narrower, more private, sideways. And as he walked, the memories began to play in his mind like ghosts. . . .

A little girl—very grave, very, very serious—playing a peleforté, singing in a clear, true voice. The first child—the first one. Almost like his own child. . . .

And then she was a slim girl of sixteen making her Final Decision: She stood before him and the others, the sunlight turning her hair into a floating black cloud that gave back no light. She wore soft white that followed the movements of her body. Her eyes were very black, very grave as they looked into his. And to him, she was beautiful. He held her hand and placed a ring on her finger, a ring with the broken symbol of infinity. She was the first. The first one. . . .

He walked the empty sideways as the sweet, the bitter memories played on: A young woman, walking with him in the woods of autumn. He had felt in awe of her a little, and envious. She seemed to know so well where she was going.

They had stopped for a while under the red leaves of a maple. The sky was very blue overhead; the air was sharp with a cool tang that tasted of minerals and arctic ice.

They entered a small ravine, crushing bright leaves under their feet, half-running, half-sliding down to the banks of a shining stream that hopped from rock to rock and sent curling plumes of spray into the air. They walked precariously along its edge until the stream slid away down the face of a broad smooth stone that slanted into a little pool below it.

There the forest opened and Blood Mountain struggled against the sky in the distance. She stopped then under a dark hemlock and broke off a twig, crushing the needles between her fingers, sniffing deeply. "I love this scent, Kurt. To me, it is the essence of Renascence, clean and wild." She held the broken twig under his nose.

The pungent scent brought back to him a time very long ago—a Christmas tree, a small boy held close in loving arms. The world had been newly minted then, and to him, nothing had been so sharply etched, so sweet as that, until now. He kissed her then, and held her, held her as if to let go would be to die.

He ran his hands over her slim body, stripping it of clothes, reveling in the touch of the familiar curves and hollows of her, the smell of her, the taste. They clung together, as if by clinging they could be one creature, one throbbing, feeling, touching creature. And when his shuddering climax came, he couldn't draw away. Not yet. It wasn't enough. Not enough. Not ever enough.

And when they drew apart at last and pulled on clothes aflame with dying leaves, he reached out and touched her hair, her throat. "Come with me. Come live with me, Tanya. I need you."

She didn't answer just then. She stood and reached out a hand to him. He took it. And the sun shone on their two hands and sparkled on the broken gold figure on the ring she wore. She held his face between her hands then and looked at it. And after that, she dropped her arms to her sides and turned away. She stared through the flaming leaves at the mountains for a long time before she said, "We walk on different paths, Kurt. Mine is here."

And he looked at her and found her beautiful.

As the years passed, he saw her age. As the years lined her face and streaked her hair with white, he came often to Renascence. He listened to her music and to her soft voice. They walked in the woods together in soft spring rains while small birds sang. They walked in summer and in the crisp frosts of October. They walked against the icy winds of winter, and he found her beautiful.

And then when she became too old, too infirm, for their walks together, he still came, but not as often. And they sat together in the warmth of her cabin, drinking wild tea sweetened with honey. She smiled and reached out, ruffling his hair in a teasing way as she would a son, or a grandson. For the first time he saw how frail she was, how fragile. *I'm going to watch you die. I'm going to live and watch you die.*

He kissed her then, gently, like a son. He said, "Goodbye," and then he left, shutting the cabin door softly behind him.

He had not been back to Renascence since then.

Chapter 9

A sick anger budded and bloomed inside David as he watched the hover land at Renascence and discharge its cargo of smooth-faced immortals into the sun. They congregated in the clearing, these people of rank and importance. They had given up a day or two of forever to come to the funeral of the woman who had amused them with her music and her life.

He hated them for it. He watched them group in little clumps and knots in the clearing, renewing acquaintance, laughing, conversing.

His hands drew into fists. "Damn them," he said aloud.

Liss's hand touched his, running softly across the tense skin over his knuckles.

Another hover came into sight over the treetops. It slowed and dropped to a gentle landing.

"It's a novelty, isn't it?" he said bitterly. "They all want to come to death rites. It gives them a thrill."

She fingered the little amethyst on the gold chain around her neck. "That isn't fair, David," she said. "They've come to show the respect they had for her. She wasn't just another mortal artist, you know. She was special. She was the first mortal."

"The first mortal?"

Liss sighed faintly. "You don't know much about her, do you?"

He snorted, "Only every piece of music she ever wrote."

"I'm not talking about her music, David."

74

He looked at her, puzzled. It had never entered his head that Tanya Rolfe could be considered apart from her music. It was as if the two were so intertwined that trying to separate them would be useless, senseless.

"She was the first mortal," said Liss evenly, "the first to deny immortality. She came here over ninety years ago, David. Imagine how alone she must have felt—being the first. She designed the ring all of you wear. Did you know that?"

He shook his head. He was acutely conscious of her phrase, "the ring all of you wear." Liss's Final Decision wasn't until tomorrow, and yet she had already drawn herself away from him, aligned herself with the throng in the clearing. Somehow this cutting off of herself hurt him more than anything else. After a minute he said stiffly, "I suppose you learned all that when you wrote her obituary."

A look of surprise crossed her face, then a faint smile. "I've been here five years too, David. Tanya Rolfe and I were friends. We used to talk." She looked away for a moment, remembering. "We didn't talk about her music much at all. I didn't know enough to talk about that. We talked about feelings, about loneliness—things like that."

"I didn't know that. I thought—"

"Oh, look!" Liss jumped to her feet and ran toward the passengers disembarking from the second hover. David stood, watching her run, watching her reach out to the big dark-haired man. They embraced and then they were coming toward him, Liss leading, tugging the big man along. He was smiling down at her. He wore the rank of office, but he was still too far away for David to make out the order of the colors.

"David," called Liss. "Look who's here." She looked up proudly at the stranger.

He had dark good looks, this man, and a slight sardonic twist to his lips. He was well-muscled and looked no more than thirty.

"David, this is Uncle Kurt." She reached out and took David's hand. "He's not really my uncle, but I've called him that since I could talk."

David stood dumbly by. His hand lay limp in Liss's grasp. He felt like a child before this aggressively male stranger who

wore the colors he now recognized. The man was Kurt Kraus
—the Minister of Culture. And he was over two hundred
years old.

Kurt Kraus cupped Liss's face in his hands and looked
down at her. "You've grown up, little one."

David felt his lips compress at the happy look on her face.

The man smiled in his direction and reached out a hand
to him. Reluctantly, David stretched out his hand—with the
black and gold ring. At the sight of it, a look passed through
Kurt's eyes that David couldn't read.

"So you're staying on at Renascence," said the man.

"David's a musician," Liss said proudly. "He was Tanya
Rolfe's protégé."

The look again—what was it? Then it was gone. "You
must play for me sometime, David."

David nodded, not speaking. He'd never play for him.
Never. Not for this man who looked at Liss so familiarly. He
knew he was overreacting, but he couldn't seem to help it—
he didn't really want to.

"Your last name is Defour, isn't it?" asked Kurt.

He nodded stiffly.

"You have immortal parents, then. But you'll lose your
crib name soon enough. It's a fine thing to meet your parents
and take their name. When you join the Society of Adults,
you'll see. It's the biggest festival you can imagine. Food.
Vinifountains." He patted Liss on the shoulder. "You'll miss
out on all that, little one. When you're born to mortals, there's
no surprise to the big day."

"I'm not complaining. It was nice to be different and grow
up with parents," she said. "Besides, I don't have to wait to
see them. I'm going home tomorrow—back to Hoffmeir."

Kurt's brow quirked upward. His fingers pressed into her
shoulder while a look, again unreadable, crossed his face and
then was gone.

During the funeral, David and Liss sat apart. She sat with
the larger group who had not made Final Decision; he sat
across a patch of green grass and blooming daisies with a
smaller group who wore the black and gold rings.

They sat in a large semicircle. In front of them stood a platform with a casket draped in white bearing a gold embroidered broken symbol of infinity and the words, "For Art."

Tanya Rolfe's music began to play slowly. The sound swelled and grew from the parabolic shell that reflected the playing of the small orchestra. The blooming daisies began to move in a stately flow, directed by the hand of the master visiographer, Lindner.

Kurt Kraus rose and began to speak in a slow deep voice, "We are here today to celebrate the immortality of the woman, Tanya Rolfe. The music she has created in her brief span has its own life. As long as humankind continues, so will these creations continue. As long as humankind has the mind to comprehend their beauty, Tanya Rolfe does not die."

They buried her in a tiny plot of land overlooking the lake and the mountains beyond. There were nine others there.

On the next morning, before the sun was high, David slipped out of his cabin and went to the small graveyard. He carried his flute with him, nothing else.

He sat for a long time under the spreading shade of an oak tree and played. He played the music she'd written for him when he first came to Renascence: "David's Song." He played until the hover, bearing Liss away from Renascence forever, was a tiny dot in the distance.

Chapter 10

The matron wore the dark green uniform of the Colony Police. She was pudgy, and her clothes fit poorly. Her snug tunic rode in folds around her thick waist and struggled over wide hips.

She's not very bright, thought Liss McNabb. Maybe she could get away from her—when the right moment came. The thought of escape had been near the surface since they had taken her into custody on Hoffmeir the day before. It had stayed in her mind as she huddled in her locked compartment on the skiptor; and now, as she sat under the watchful stare of the matron while the Arrow sped them toward Vesta Central, the thought was paramount.

Liss changed her position slightly. The Arrow seat was uncomfortable. She felt the stares of the other passengers and self-consciously she crossed her arms in her lap in an attempt to hide her swelling belly. It was getting bigger every day—too big to deny anymore. At least she wasn't nauseated now. She had been able to get rid of the little cylinder of Neutravert that had been her constant ally since she had come home from Renascence.

A man across the aisle stared boldly at her. She glared back. Damn them all. Uneasily, she was aware of others looking at her. She might as well be wearing a sign with bright letters yelling:

No Certificate
UNAUTHORIZED PREGNANCY

Well, they weren't going to take it. It was her baby, and they could be damned. She was sick of their logic. Sick of their arguments that had turned quickly to threats. She wasn't going to be afraid of them—or their prisons.

The matron was uncommunicative, and that suited her just fine. She looked away from her and from the bold-faced man and pretended to examine the Vestan landscape as it rolled away beneath her. She sat like this, staring into the dimming Dayglow until the Arrow came to a stop in Central City.

"Off here," said the matron.

Liss stared ahead in dismay. Scarcely two blocks ahead stood the squat Corrections Center. Once they'd locked her in there, she'd never get out. Halfway there was the high-speed zont hub that connected several levels of Vesta. If she could divert the matron long enough, maybe she could get away.

They walked in silence until they came abreast of the hub. Suddenly, Liss grabbed her belly and hunched over. She began to moan.

"What is it?" asked the matron, alarm spreading over her face.

Liss grabbed the zont railing with one hand and moaned louder. She crouched by the railing.

"What's wrong? What is it?"

"The baby," she grunted through clenched teeth. "I think I'm losing the baby."

"Here?" The woman stared at Liss, bewilderment on her face. "Hurry then. It's not much farther."

In reply, Liss hunched over the rail and redoubled her moans. "Oh-o-oh! Get help. Quick!"

Hands clutching together in distress, the matron looked uncertainly at the passers-by.

"Hurry!" said Liss with a tremulous whimper. "Oh help, before it comes."

The matron turned and called, "Help." The instant the woman's back was to her, Liss leaped over the rail to the downward angling zont track below. She was running the moment her feet touched, running, diving, down the zont toward the next level.

At the foot, she stared wildly around and dashed off at an angle, running over the moving zont past a series of storage buildings. Then she turned again onto a narrow sideway, running a zigzagging path until she could run no longer.

She darted into a loading ramp and crouched in the shadows. Panting, she took huge sucking gasps of air. Her leg muscles trembled, and her heart throbbed in her ears.

She waited there until Dayglow was gone and the night of Vesta had activated the lights along the streets of the asteroid. Only then did she come out to walk cautiously along the dim sideways.

She had no idea where she would go or what she would do next. She had thought no further than the escape itself. And when she did consider it, the realization came that there was truly no way out. Vesta was large, but not that large. How would she hide? Where?

She looked very young, very uncertain, as she walked among the hulking storehouses. No one else was near—it was a place for Dayglow activity, she told herself. But to make sure, she looked around often with round blue eyes that now and then filled with moisture.

She was very tired and very hungry.

The phenomenon known as the Labyrinth crept in the wake of exhausted mine shafts. As each passage was abandoned by the robo-crushers and the men who tended them, it slowly filled with the scents of musk and sweat. The smoke from smoldering hallucinogenic oils clung to the rock of its walls, undissipated by the poor ventilation of the winding corridors. The throb of drums and bright writhing holos mingled with the scents and the smoke of the Labyrinth, luring the bored and disillusioned of the belt to its depths.

Liss stared at the dimly lit storehouses. They were full of food—and there was no way she could get to any of it. She sank exhausted at the edge of a building and leaned against it. Her stomach rumbled, and she felt the edge of hunger turn toward nausea. Maybe she could sleep. Maybe she could try and forget about the awful churning emptiness of her stomach.

A scratching sound nearby brought her to her feet. She stared toward the sound, eyes straining against the darkness. In the narrow alleyway between two storehouses a small shadow moved, stopped, then moved again. A rat! Its naked tail coiled just within a small pool of light. Rats had traveled to space early on, stowaways in man's food and supplies. The survivors had bred and multiplied until it was estimated that there were more rats than colonists now. Most of them were around the storehouses, she thought.

She began to walk again. She came to the Mining Operations and wandered among the big crushers and cutters, stumbling once in the near darkness over a projecting metal beam. Involuntary tears stung her eyes as she rubbed her bruised shin.

Eventually she came to a large mine opening. A single patch of light illuminated it. The opening was cavelike and roughly fifteen meters square. Near the opening, within the small lighted area, stood a small open shed. Just inside hung several rows of equipment. Next to a pair of protective gauntlets, Liss found a pair of goggles and reached for them, hoping they were like the ones she had played with when she was little.

She put them on. Pale shadowless light came into her eyes. The mine opening stretched ahead, gray walls meeting lighter gray dust-covered floor. She walked into the shaft.

She knew she couldn't stay here, knew they would find her by morning. And if they didn't see her first, she could be crushed by machine or incinerated by laser cutter. Yet she moved on, passing by a series of downward-leading square holes next to the walls of the mine. She peered into one. It was a straight drop, and she couldn't see the bottom. Shivering, she ventured on and looked in the next. It was the same.

She walked on until she came to the next series. This time, she spotted handholds in one of them. She looked down over the edge. The rock shaft ended about ten meters below. She had no idea where it led. But what was the choice? she asked herself.

She grasped the handhold, testing it. When it held firm, she swung a foot into a toehold and began to climb down.

It was farther than she thought to the bottom. Halfway down, she felt her legs tremble. A cramp was starting in her left calf. She clung to the handhold and looked around her. Even with the goggles, the shaft was dim. It seemed narrower than she had thought at first. It seemed to be closing in.

At the first jitters of claustrophobia, she began moving downward again.

She ran out of holds when her feet were nearly four meters from the bottom, but as she clung to the last hold and looked around, she realized that she seemed to be in one end of a narrow rock corridor. It was brighter here, too bright for the goggles. With one hand she pushed them up on her forehead and looked around.

Dim light diffused into the tunnel. The air was close and warm. Not far ahead, the passage turned to the left.

She looked at the floor below. It looked uncompromisingly hard, and much farther away than she felt comfortable about even in the low gravity.

Her arms ached, and the muscles in her calf were beginning to twitch again. She pressed her belly against the rock of the shaft. Her knuckles showed white on the handholds. Sweat began to bead her forehead, causing the goggles to begin to slide. She was too tired to climb up again. She couldn't. She'd have to jump.

She eased her toes to the edge of their foothold and extending her arms dropped into a squatting position. Her hands, slimed with sweat, lost traction on the metal holds. She had to jump before she fell.

She jumped, legs bent, fell awkwardly, and landed with one foot turned under. She gasped at the hot agony in her foot and ankle, and thrusting her head back, she strained against the pain.

She closed her eyes and knotted her fists until she felt the initial wave subside to a heavy throb. Nothing was left but hopelessness.

"Come with me," said a voice like velvet.

Her eyes flew open; her heart lodged in her throat. There was no one in the corridor.

"*Come with me,*" the voice repeated.

She looked around wildly.

Suddenly, overhead a light flickered, winked, swirled like blue gauze, and then extended itself into a shape—a cross. "*Come with me . . . A better life . . . Come with me . . .*"

The cross began to blaze with a cold white light. "*Silver T . . .*" it whispered. "*Silver T. . . .*"

The holo swirled over her head. "*Come with me.*" As it spoke, it shimmered, dissolved and spread its gauzy net toward her. She shrank against the rock wall. The holo regrouped into the cross. "*Come with me . . . A better life . . . Come with me . . .*"

The holo fluttered away on its programmed course and disappeared. Liss stared at the empty passage ahead. Where was she? Worse, who was out there? She managed to get to her feet. Her ankle was beginning to swell badly, but she didn't think it was broken. When she gingerly tried to put her weight on it, pain stabbed and ran up to her knee. But if she ignored the worst of it, she found she could hobble a little.

She looked around once more. There were two choices. She could stay in this dead-end corridor with no place to hide and nothing to eat or drink, or she could see what lay at the end of the passage.

Leaning against the rough wall, she began to make her painful way down the corridor. When she reached the end, she peeped cautiously around. The passage led on, angling to the right and slightly downhill. No one was there.

The going was rougher now as she picked her way over the uneven floor. Once, she slipped on a greasy layer of stone and caught herself heavily. The pain in her ankle took her breath away. She leaned against the wall for support and felt the sweat grow on her forehead and trickle down her face.

The blue light fluttered into the corridor again. She stared at it, blinking as it whispered and cajoled. "*. . . A better life . . .*" it promised as it swooped and turned and blazed its cross-shape at her. "*. . . Silver T . . .*" and fluttered away once again.

Smells and sounds began to filter into the passage. Just ahead, the corridor turned again sharply to the right. She

slowly thrust her head around the wall. Blood-red disembod-
ied eyes stared into hers. She gasped and shrank back.

Only a holo, she told herself firmly. She heard a cooing
laugh and looked again. A chubby naked baby boy floated in
the passage. He laughed and held out his arms to her. And as
he laughed, his penis grew giant and erect and the soft baby
lines of his face contorted into a screeching gargoyle. The
holo faded, rippled, winked out.

A shiver traced its way up her spine. She had never heard
of the Labyrinth. If anyone had told her, she would have
scoffed in disbelief. The corridor she had come to was wide,
curving out of sight a few meters further on. The sounds and
the smells were growing more distinct. Just across from her in
the wall near the floor, a square hole yawned. The opening
was about a meter wide. Making sure no one was in sight, she
hobbled across and looked inside.

It was totally dark in there. She pulled the goggles down
over her eyes. With them on, the hole became the opening to
a tunnel of rock lasered to a glasslike smoothness.

Suddenly, she realized that the noise level around the
bend of the corridor had increased. She could hear individual
voices. She couldn't let them find her. Heart beating fast,
wincing from the pain in her ankle, she backed into the
tunnel.

She eased herself just inside as the holo baby began to
laugh again. Its screech echoed inside the tunnel. And there
was another noise too—footsteps—and they were coming
closer.

Instinctively, she backed further into the tunnel. The
moment she did, she felt the passage dip abruptly. Gasping,
she began to slide.

She slid rapidly, turning toward the right once. Near the
bottom the chute leveled, slowing her descent.

She landed in back of a large, dim room hewn from rock.
With a start, she realized that it was full of people—dozens of
people—staring toward something in the center of the room.

Her heart pressed and pounded in her throat. Then, suddenly, she realized that no one had noticed her. She drew
back against the wall, listening to the drone of indistinguish-

able voices, seeing the gray shapes that swayed in rhythmic motion from side to side. Gray against gray, they moved as if they were one body.

Gray against gray. Of course! She pulled the goggles from her eyes and looked again. She was plunged into darkness. No wonder they hadn't seen her. There was no light except at the center of the room. There, a shallow metal dish a meter across flickered with bluish flame. Its heavy scent gradually crept across the room toward her, bearing a smell not unlike the honeysuckle of Renascence—but something else too—beneath the sweet smell was an underlay, a scent she dimly remembered. What was it?

She eased herself back in the opening of the chute and watched. The scent tickled her mind with hints of fairy tale and nightmare. Why? Then she remembered. She had been only eight or nine when the big boy offered it to her. He had lighted the tiny shallow spoon of oil and wafted it under her nose. And he had laughed. Laughed as she cried and flinched when the trolls came into her head—and the fearful witch riding a giant green dragon with flame for breath that flickered over her hair and set it agonizingly aflame. He had laughed.

She held her breath involuntarily, but when she breathed again, she realized that the scent was faint. Faint, but definite.

She pulled the goggles over her eyes again and looked around. The room played its drama in shades of gray against ash. The people sat in a concentric circle around the smouldering dish. They sat on the floor with outstretched arms linked, and their upper bodies swayed in a slow, a rhythmic ellipse. And as she watched them, she realized that they were children. The oldest was probably no more than fourteen; the youngest only ten or so.

Something flared in the center of the smoking dish. The light nearly blinded her. She snatched the goggles away. When her eyes adjusted, she saw a fountain of blue flame playing above the dish, leaping toward the high ceiling, splashing its cold fire over the room, over the staring children.

The background hum grew louder and sorted itself into a litany—a sibilant hiss, then a whispered murmur stroked her ears: "S'sss . . . fur'rrr . . . t'eeee . . ." What did it mean?

Her head began to ache as the sound, as the insinuating scent, as the flame that burned now blue, now white, played against her senses.

The blue flame spun in an arc above the center of the dish, its whispered circle changing now to a disc, and then a sphere. The colors shifted in the globe, blue swirling into white, and as it hung and slowly turned, she saw the pattern —Earth.

Then just above the moving globe, a silver cross appeared and drove its heavy shaft straight through the axis of the sphere. The oceans of the Earth splashed out in liquid blue and then the body of the globe broke up and crumbled into dust.

"Obey . . . Obey . . ."

She heard them say it then and thought she saw, for just a flashing moment, a confusing cherub-smile atop the cross.

"Obey . . . Obey . . ."

The children moved as one thing in the room.

"Rewards forever . . ." whispered from the walls.

And then two men came. They brought a boy between them—a boy with glazing eyes and vacant face—a boy they handled like a doll.

They stood him up against a cross and tied him there.

She watched with burning eyes and fogging mind. What were they doing to him? What? And why?

And when the two men moved away, she saw the boy's head flopping on a limber neck that seemed awry.

They raised him on the cross.

"From death—reward."

She stared as a projection grew—the boy's face, smiling down.

"From death—reward."

She stared. "Oh God! His neck. He's killed. Oh God!"

She screamed and screamed and screamed without knowing that she was the only one who did.

Chapter 11

The lines of Kurt Kraus's face were drawn heavy with anger. "What happened to her?"

Deputy Minister Silvio Tarantino raised both hands, palm down, as if to smooth troubled waters. "An unfortunate incident. After the girl ran away from the matron, she hid in an area near the central zontilator hub. Some of our children are attracted to the hub. It's exciting for them to play there. Of course, we forbid it, but that does tend to make it more enticing, doesn't it?" He smiled ruefully and shook his head. "The boy was running on top of the upper railing. He lost his balance and fell. Broken neck. He died instantly.

"The McNabb girl saw it all. She tried to run to him and she fell too. She was hysterical when she was found. I'm told her hysteria was intensified due to the drugs."

"Drugs?" There was something about the man Kurt needed to remember, something buried in a clot of old memories. Something. . . .

"She had taken an hallucinogenic some time before."

Kurt narrowed his eyes. "I never knew her to take drugs."

"She was distraught. People often do strange things when they are under stress," he said smoothly. "There are witnesses, of course, if you'd care to talk with them."

"I'm sure there are," he said shortly. There was something about the man that set Kurt on guard. It was his manner. He was too glib, too easy with a phrase, too ingenuous— the mark of either an exceptionally honest man, or a profes-

87

sional liar. Kurt leveled a stare at Tarantino. He didn't doubt his professionalism for a moment. "How is she now?"

The man met his look with an open, almost cherubic gaze, yet the birthmark at the angle of his jaw ticked with the clenching and unclenching of his jaw. "Doing well, I understand. They've given her something to help her sleep."

"And her baby?"

"Still here. We canceled the procedure when we learned of your, uh, interest in the matter." Even the subtly inserted pause seemed calculated. It implied a slightly raised eyebrow. Why, after all, should the Minister of Culture be so interested in a schoolgirl?

Kurt stood up abruptly. "I want to see her."

"Of course," said the little man.

Acting on impulse, Kurt made a short detour on his way to Liss. Entering Communications Control, he commandeered a terminal in the name of the Ministry.

The soft voice of the communicator spoke in his ear: "How can we assist you, Mr. Kraus?"

"Request bio-sketch, Silvio Tarantino, Deputy Minister, Vesta."

He stared at the information, hoping to jog loose the nagging scrap of memory:

TARANTINO, SILVIO ANTHONY: Born M-G 17, New Providence Island, Consolidated Bahamian Sector, Earth.
Father: Victor Luis Tarantino, deceased M-G 29.
Mother: Caterina "Kitty" Theresa Martez Tarantino, deceased M-G 57.
Dormitory: Victoria, N.P. M-G 17–35.
Studies: Acad. of the Azores M-G 35–39.
    Spec. Studies WorldCo ComSchool M-G 39–41.
Immigrated Vesta M-G 41. . . .

Nothing. Kurt scanned the sketch again. Nothing at all familiar. And yet he couldn't shake the feeling that there was something very wrong here.

"Complete bio, Tarantino, Silvio Anthony," he said. When the communicator complied, he studied it carefully. To his disgust, he learned nothing.

Liss was sleeping when Kurt walked into her room. She lay curled on her side with her arms folded over her face, palm out, as if to ward off a blow. When he walked across the room, she stirred and muttered and then lay quiet.

He sat by her bedside and looked at her. Her face was dirty and streaked with dried tears. She looked very young and very vulnerable. The thin bedcover followed the convex line of her belly. It had been over four months—four months since she had left Renascence. And the boy who was responsible didn't even know.

She moaned and pressed her lips together.

Stubborn, thought Kurt, stubborn even in her sleep. Too stubborn to see the cost of what she had done. She needs to be spanked, he thought agressively. He could still see the anguish in her parents' faces when they told him. And Sean . . . Sean had tried to be light about it, even making a feeble joke or two, but the concern he felt for this girl who carried his genes after four generations, the love he felt had etched his face with lines of worry and shadowed his eyes.

And they were the only family he had—his adopted little brother Sean, and this girl, and her parents. Everyone else was dead long ago. "Stubborn little girl," he said softly. She didn't know the cost.

Liss turned and whimpered in her sleep. She flung her hands away from her face. Her eyes were open, staring at nothing. "Oh no. Oh, God! Awful, awful, awful—" She began to scream.

He was at her side in a moment, holding her, petting her, talking nonsense in quiet, soothing tones, "There, there. All right. There, there," until she grew quiet.

Then she blinked and looked at him as if he had not been there until now. Surprise widened her eyes. "Uncle Kurt? Oh, it was awful. So awful—" She struggled to a sitting position.

He took her hand between his. "What was awful? What happened to you?"

She looked at him thoughtfully, then stared at her knees. When she looked back at him, puzzlement spread over her face. "I don't remember, Uncle Kurt. I don't remember at all."

He looked at her strangely. Then he began to talk of other things, inconsequential things, until she said, "You came to get me out of trouble, didn't you?"

"I came to do what I could do."

"I knew you'd understand," she said, clasping his hand. "I knew you would."

"Did you?" He shook his head. "I understand that you managed to acquire an illegal pregnancy as a going-away present from a young Renascence musician. I understand that you have parceled a very large ration of grief on your family and yourself. And I understand that you completely failed to cooperate with the Population authorities."

"They wanted to take my baby."

"And so they will. And after they do that, they will confine you in a Vestan prison. Is that what you want?"

She caught her lower lip between her teeth and looked at him for a long time before she said, "But you can help me, Uncle Kurt."

"And you're counting on that."

"I guess I am."

The corner of his lip quirked in a smile devoid of humor. "I suppose I should be flattered at the simple belief you have in my omnipotence."

Alarm darted across her face. "You can, can't you?"

He looked away for a moment. When he looked back, something shadowed his eyes. "For the sake of this discussion, let's consider that there may be something I can do."

A look of relief. "Oh, I knew it."

He caught her hands. "Why did you do it, Liss? You're not stupid. You knew what you were doing."

"I had to."

"Had to?"

"Yes." She pulled her hands away and wrapped them around her knees. "Because of David."

"You love him?"

"Yes. But that's not why. Not all of it."

"Why, then?"

"Because he's staying at Renascence. Because he's going to live and die there. He'll never marry, have children, even though he can. And all of him shouldn't die, Uncle Kurt. At least, that's the way I see it."

So that was the reason. She was offering this boy a kind of immortality—and he didn't even know. Kurt leaned back and stared at the ceiling, partly to think, partly to hide the look of pain he felt creep over his face and tug at the corners of his mouth. He had been afraid that this might be her reason; and when he heard it, he knew there would be no changing her mind. He remembered the two of them standing on the hillside at Renascence when he had come for Tanya Rolfe's funeral. Did she carry the germ of David's child then? He thought of the pain in the boy's face when he looked at her and took her hand in his, twining his long fingers through hers. But he wore a ring, and she didn't. He wore a gold ring with the broken symbol of infinity that caught in the sunlight and glinted like the gold in Liss's hair.

Kurt dropped his eyes to hers, "Will you give up the baby?"

"No."

"Your offense is against Population. The Minister of Population does not take orders from me."

"But, you could get him to agree. You could make a b—" She stopped at the look on his face.

"You were going to suggest that I bargain with Population—make a trade. Well, I have, Liss," he said slowly. "I have."

She hugged him, "Oh thank you. I knew you could help."

"You haven't heard the terms."

Her eyebrows raised in a question.

"I can offer you a term-contract of marriage."

"With David?"

"No. David is a minor without rights. Your contract will be with me. Legally binding for twenty years."

A smile twitched at the corner of her mouth. "But I've always called you uncle. Isn't that incestuous?" She began to giggle and then to laugh until lines crinkled the corners of her eyes and tears filled them. "I'm sixteen," she whooped, "and I'm going to marry an older man."

He had intended to be stern, but watching her laugh proved infectious. He grinned at her and gave her a paternal kiss on the forehead, which served to increase her giggles.

It wasn't until after she sank back exhausted on the bed and dozed off that the doubts came flooding back. Ndebele had been most polite, most considerate when Kurt had outlined Liss's problem to him. The Minister of Population had offered to be most cooperative about issuing a permit and a term-contract license. "And, of course," he had said, "Population would expect certain concessions from Culture. There was the troublesome matter of the mentally defective children. Now, if Renascence would accept these children. . . ."

And he had said—God help him—he had said, "Yes."

He stared at the girl as she turned and muttered in her sleep and threw her arms over her face and cried out, "Awful, awful, awful. Oh God! Awful. . . ."

PART
TWO

Two Years Later

Chapter 1

The starship hung in the black of space just off Vesta. A faraway sun glinted on the silver ellipse that would carry thirty thousand people on her maiden voyage.

The ship was nearly finished, with only the final fittings left for the technicians who swarmed her hull like sperm and breached her virgin depths.

She bore the name ARIES on her hull and on her bridge. She carried the Ramirez star drive in her bowels. She bore the name Aries, but they called her "the Ram."

They entered the ship through the starboard bay and debarked through a pressurized tunnel that led to a large sublif. "Feels like Earth's gravity," said Kurt Kraus.

"Yes," answered Jacoby, "but only in the outer levels. The Ram is spinning on her longitudinal axis. The pull decreases as we move inboard." Jacoby punched a code, and they began to move. "You'll find Central Habitat's gravity more like Vesta's. I think you'll be impressed with Central Hab," said the foreman with obvious pride.

The sublif accelerated, then decelerated with stomach-lurching suddenness. They stepped out into what seemed to be a large public building. "This way," said Jacoby. Kurt followed the man to a large landscaped square with a central fountain. He looked around at the sight in amazement. He stood in a village studded with low buildings interspersed with shrubbery and trees. A zont hub ringed the square and splayed out in all directions. In the distance along the zont lines, Kurt could see more low buildings amid green fields and young trees.

The horizon curved upward in the distance. He felt as if he stood at the bottom of a huge basin. Overhead an irregular blue "sky," reflecting the blue rooftops below it and ringed with green, startled him.

The foreman grinned. "Sky Lake," he said. "Incredible effect isn't it?" He swung his arm overhead, pointing toward the left of the blue. "Up there is the Park—with a capital P. Although we have recreational parks in this hemi, the Park is special. It's a place to go—a different place."

Kurt nodded. For thirty thousand people enclosed in a space-going egg some twenty kilometers across, it was essential that they have diversion—someplace different to see, someplace different to be.

"The plan is to let over half of it grow wild and to allow only a limited number on the trails at a given time. Of course, it's not very wild yet." He grinned. "The trees and shrubs are young, but the soil's good. And in a subtropical climate, trees grow fast. Gumbo limbo and mahogany make up the bulk of them." He swung his arm in an arc over his head and pointed to the right of Sky Lake. "Up there is the place you'll want to see—New Renascence. The best way to get there is to go back one level and take the Hemichute."

Kurt followed Jacoby through the maze of sublifs and passageways that led to the Hemichute. Everywhere he looked, work parties swarmed over the ship. Most of the workers knew Jacoby and called him by name. They reserved curious stares, some bordering on insolence, for Kurt.

He took a seat in the Hemi beside Jacoby. As the car accelerated, he considered the man who sat next to him. Although Jacoby had spent years on Earth, he had been born on Vesta and so was acceptable to the colony crews who built the Ram. Jacoby's ability was one of the few things the colonists and the Earthers agreed on, thought Kurt. The Ram had failed to create the camaraderie the Ministry had hoped for. The tension between the colonies and Earth had grown.

Needed ore shipments were consistently delayed due to "un-avoidable accident." Mislabeled cargo was time and again shunted to the wrong destination, there to be buried under Vestan red tape.

When the Ministry looked into the matter, its investiga-tors found themselves in the worst accommodations in the belt. They were beset with transportation "breakdowns," "malfunctioning computers," and bland-faced colonists with obsequious apologies for "stupid mistakes." They found their beds lumpy and their food cold. They did not doubt for a moment that the treatment they received was deliberate, and when they complained to the Deputy Minister's office, they were met with polite but blank stares and an increasing string of "unfortunate accidents." As a result, the Minister of Com-merce was coming that day to Vesta to head a serious investi-gation.

Other visitors from Earth had not fared much better than the Ministry envoys. Lately there had been a number of thefts and physical attacks. Each event taken separately could be, and was, explained facilely by the Deputy Minister's office. Taken cumulatively, the pattern was obvious. Jacoby had to be aware of it.

Kurt asked him so—directly.

He got a surprisingly direct answer. "You're right. When I was a boy, we always felt mildly contemptuous of Earthers, but it was always tempered with good humor—you know, the Earther-joke mental set." He paused, staring outside the car as it sped through a clump of buildings on the Ram's periph-ery. "I've been away a long time. When I came back, I could feel the difference at once. The contempt is still there, but the humor's gone now."

"Do you know why?"

Jacoby shook his head. "I try to stay out of it. I consider myself to be apolitical."

Kurt pressed him. "But you've worked directly with these men. You must have your own ideas about what's hap-pening."

"Ideas don't count for much when the ground under your feet begins to move."

"What do you mean?"

"I was in an avalanche once, in the Andes. It begins small, you know. If you stand around wondering how it began, you'll earn a quick, cold grave. The thing to do is get out of the way."

Kurt felt the car decelerate. When it stopped, the two men got out. In a few minutes they stood in a stand of young trees by the shore of Sky Lake. Far overhead, the buildings of the village clustered. Maybe later, thought Kurt. Later, when the trees have grown maybe it will be more like an Earth place. Maybe even now, at night. He tried to imagine darkness in this place, at the shore of this shallow lake. Would the lights of the village look like stars overhead?

He looked at the foreman, "What are your plans when you're finished here?"

"I'm going with her," said Jacoby. "I'm going with the Ram."

Kurt returned to Vesta by shuttle. When he reached the Ministry guest quarters, the lobby was clogged with police and media personnel. He found himself staring into a three-vee camera, "Do you have any comment, Citizen Kraus, concerning the tragedy?"

He pushed man and camera aside with a quick "no comment," and turned to an aide. "Walk with me," he said in a low voice. The two men walked to a nearby alcove away from the crowd. "What happened?"

"The Minister of Commerce," said the aide in a whisper. "He went up to rest before his meeting with Silvio Tarantino. When he didn't return, they checked. He's dead. Murdered. His neck was broken."

Kurt stared at the man. Not murdered, he thought. Assassinated. There was a difference—a world of difference.

Liss's hand brushed lightly over his neck, and he felt a pleasing prickle shiver over his nape. He looked at her. Her hair was caught in the red glow of the sun sinking into the Gulf as it sent its last rays over the little Florida island.

"You were staring at the water as if you were never going

to see it again," she said. Her eyes crinkled at the edges in
amusement. "I've heard of 'eyes drinking it in,' but I've never
seen such a graphic example. I thought the tide was going
out, but you're the cause."

He looked at her thoughtfully. Pretty little girl. Friend.
The sun washed her skin with pink and glowed along the
curving lines of her body. A breeze caught her hair, lifting it
in little strands that rode the wind like pale curling feathers.
He felt a hot desire for her go through him like an electric
shock. He shook his head once, as if to clear it, and strode
across the narrow beach into the cool water.

He swam out to a sandbar where small breakers rolled.
The sand felt smooth under his feet, and he stood precariously
balanced in the surf. Then he turned toward the shore and
looked at her again. She was on her knees, running her hands
through a tide pool, turning rosy shells over and holding them
to the light.

She was a child. There were centuries between them—a
gulf greater than this one that washed between the shores of
Florida and Mexico. He balanced between the breakers and
the turning tide. Small particles of sand churned in the waters
around him, a small fish swam against his leg, a momentary
dark streak that vanished in the surf.

He began to swim. Buoyant in the salty water, he swam a
hundred meters to a jetty that sent small whirlpools around its
barnacle-rough pilings. He hung on, riding the buffeting of
the water, then releasing his grip, swam again until, fatigued,
he waded toward the shore, emerging with the water running
from him in salty rivers.

Liss handed him a thick towel, warm from the sand. "Did
you swim up an appetite?"

He toweled dry and then, in the last light of the dying
sunset, examined the shells she had collected, running his
thumb over each smooth inner surface. Listening to the drum
of the low waves, feeling the foam run over his feet and wash
away again, he thought of another shore. He thought of a
shallow lake in a starship called the Ram, a silent lake whose
waters would never feel the pull of the moon or the shift of
tide.

"The Ram needs someone like you," Gerstein had told him. "Someone to lead the voyage." To leave Earth. To leave this sun forever. To travel in a hurtling cocoon toward other suns. And some day—perhaps—to lay a footprint on another shore.

"Hungry?" she asked again.

He looked up. "Thank you for meeting me here, Liss."

"Of course," she said.

They ate their dinner on a wide veranda. Insects beat against its invisible walls, fell back, flew again toward the light of the candles on their table. The Ministry house squatted on a low dune amid broad sea grapes and hibiscus bushes that closed their red flowers against the night. Below the dune, across the little beach, the dark tide rolled and froth showed white in the moonlight.

They ate coquina soup and avocado salad and broiled snapper from the Gulf and sipped a chilled white wine with a flinty taste to it. They praised the wine and the fish, and then they fell silent.

Liss looked at the dark water, at the foaming spray that leaped at the moon as he watched her. Little friend, he thought, you have lines of worry on your face. Aloud, he said, "Have your studies gone well? Your work?"

The lines smoothed away. She smiled, "I'm progressing. The ancient craft of journalism suits me, I guess. And you? And your work?"

"It goes on." He reached across the table and took her hand. It was warm in his. He turned it over and held it, palm up, and stared into it.

She laughed. "Are you going to tell my fortune?"

"I believe I will," he said. He traced a line on her palm. "Here—a long life. A very long life."

"Amazing," she said. "What else do you see?"

"Here"—he touched again—"I see a child."

Her hand turned slightly in his; she looked away.

"And here, I see a legal contract, to a much older man."

She looked back at him then, an eyebrow tilting quizzically.

"And here I see diverging paths." He began to speak more

rapidly now, holding her hand lightly in his. "I see other in-
terests, here, for you. Other people. Young men. You should
try that, you know."

Her hand felt cold in his. She pulled it away. "Maybe
you're right. Maybe I will."

He had expected it, asked for it. Why did he feel an emptiness when she agreed?

She stood up in a few minutes. "I'm tired. I think I'll go
to bed."

He spread his hands on the table, studying them, making no move to get up. "I suppose you'll be leaving in the
morning."

"I suppose I will," she said. "Goodnight."

Her room was next to his. He lay on his bed and heard
her move on her bed, lie still and move again. And then he
heard a catching, sobbing sound. A pause, and then again.

He sat on the side of his bed and clutched his knees, and
when the sound went on, he got up and went to her room.
The door was unlocked. He pushed it open and went to her.
The room was dark with only the light of the moon to see by.
He touched her shoulder. "What, Liss? What is it?"

Her face was buried in her hands. He sat by her and
gently pulled her hands away. Her tears were glistening tracks.
"What is it?" he asked again.

"N-nothing." But she began to sob. Finally she lay quiet,
and then she said, "People should have someone. Someone
who matters."

He stroked her hair. "I know."

"I don't have anybody." She rubbed her wet cheek with
the back of her hand. "I want my baby, Kurt. I don't want her
to be in a dorm. I want her. I want Alani." She began to cry
again.

He held her as if she were a little girl. He held her and
patted her until the moon was gone and she slept. He held
her and listened as the surf boomed on the dark beach.

Chapter 2

The salt wind whipped David's hair into his eyes. He stood on a narrow beach and squinted out over the sparkling water. The surf boomed and echoed, roiling up the beach to send its chilly foam over his feet, then running back to sea.

He reached into his pack and took out a tiny recorder. Checking its meters, he set dials and pushed buttons automatically. The little machine had almost become part of him —an electronic extension of David Defour. He had used it nearly every day for the two years since Final Decision. The infrasonic tracing blipping its way across a minute screen was the one reality that held his life together.

A curved line on the horizon became a disc, then became a small two-seater hover. It came in fast, skimming the waves like a flat stone skipping over a pond. It slowed when it was nearly overhead, then all forward movement stopped and it dropped gently to the sandy beach. The hatch opened, and the biggest man David had ever seen got out.

His name was Jonathan Long.

Startled, David stared at the man. Jonathan was huge in stature, like a broad and blowing great whale. Like the whales that he felt kin to, his great bulk was cased in blubber, rolling tides of flesh and blubber.

And from the center of that being shone a soul of gentle brightness, through dark eyes that radiated warmth. His voice boomed like storm surf. "Hello, David."

The sound washed over him. The whale man, he

thought. He's like them. He really is. The wet sand beneath
his heels melted away and he took a quick step to save his
balance.

"I see you're ready," said Jonathan. "Let's go."

David nodded and followed the giant man to the hover.
In a minute, they rose straight up no more than five meters
and headed out toward open water.

Jonathan handled the controls with a delicacy David
wouldn't have believed possible if he hadn't seen it for himself.
The man's bulging fingers touched a lever; the craft banked
suddenly and changed direction.

David stared at the man's hands. He wore no ring.

Jonathan caught the look and laughed, "This hasn't been
on my hand for the last seventy or so kilos." He touched his
shirt front and pulled out the black and gold ring that dangled
from a chain around his neck. "My fingers got too big for it.
Even the little finger. So, now tell me," he boomed, "what
brings about your interest in whales?"

"I'm a musician—" David began.

"And you want to use whale song in your music? Well,
son, I'm afraid it's all been done. Long ago."

"No, it hasn't. Not what I'm doing."

Jonathan gave him a quick look. "And what's that?"

"I'll show you." David rummaged in his pack and pulled
out the recorder. He fitted it with a small silver disc and
switched it on. The haunting song of the humpback whale
began. As it ended, another began, similar, but definitely
changed. "You see, it's different."

"Of course it's different. Whales are intelligent. Inven-
tive. Their song is proof of that."

"Maybe that's why nobody bothered to look any farther.
I want you to hear something else." He slipped another disc
into the little machine. It was lower pitched and repetitive,
but otherwise similar to the creaking notes of the first song.

"Now, listen." David adjusted the machine and played
the disc again. It was higher pitched this time, almost identical
with parts of the first song, but other parts—the high pinging
notes, the drawn-out melodic squeals—were missing. "Do
you know what that is?"

"One track of a multi-track whale song recording," said Jonathan.

"I think so, too," said David, "only there weren't any whales within hundreds of miles when this was recorded."

Jonathan didn't speak for a moment. They skimmed over the open water with the waves leaping up from below, nearly touching the hover. Spray misted the plexishield. As soon as the washers wiped it away, another coating sprayed over the surface. Finally, the man said, "All right, David. You have my curiosity aroused."

David grinned. "I think part of the whale's song is altered infrasound. That's what that last tape was—the sound of the rocks of their breeding ground—little quivers of the tectonic plates. I've been collecting these tapes for two years. I think whales sense infrasound and transpose it up several octaves. I think they use it to tell each other how to find food."

Jonathan blew a skeptical breath through pursed lips. "Not possible. They use echolocation for that. Not infrasound at all. Ultrasonics."

"Yes. To locate plankton layers and so on. But how do the other whales know where that plankton is? How do they know, for that matter, how to navigate through thousands of miles of open ocean?"

Jonathan stared at him, and then a slow grin spread over his massive face. "Sort of a '*ping, ping*' plankton's here between these '*creak, creak*' rocks. Is that what you're saying?"

"Close. Every mountain and trench in the sea makes a different infrasound. I think whales imitate the sound to describe the place." David laughed, "Something like—'they're serving a good meal back at the grunt-groan. Turn left at the creak.' They couldn't do that with echolocation alone, could they?"

"Well, if one whale is feeding, another could spot him with ultrasound," Jonathan began.

"But, what about later? After that first whale left the area? How else could he give the other whales the message? I think it must be infrasound language. What do you think?" he asked Jonathan. "You're the expert."

"Me?" Jonathan's hands sat lightly on the controls. "I'm

not an expert, David. I'm a bum. A whale bum. You don't
know what that means, do you—that term? It's archaic for
drone."

His eyes widened, "You have to be the expert."

"Have to be? I don't have to be anything, David. The
government sees to that." He touched the chain at his neck.
"With this ring, I can have anything I want—all I have to do
is die for it."

"But—" David began. Then he stopped. He didn't know
what to say.

"Oh, I started off with big plans, big hopes," said Jonathan. "But, somehow I got dislodged from those plans after
my Final Decision. I was going to be a biologist. Study those
big blubbers out there." A rueful smile slipped across his face.
"I'm not sure what happened. Depression, I guess. I began to
doubt. I'd chosen to die for science. Trouble is, for me it died
first."

"So you aren't—I mean, you don't—"

"I chase whales, David. All over the world. I haven't had
an original thought in twenty years." He slid the hover around
in a banking turn. David felt his stomach lurch.

"But now," said Jonathan. "Tell me about yourself. How
are you going to use this infrasound in your music?"

He felt sick. He didn't know how to answer. He looked at
the big man sitting next to him, and he felt hot shame.

At least Jonathan was honest. Honest enough to admit
what he hadn't admitted to himself. What he hadn't dared to
admit. Now he couldn't lie to himself any longer. Gathering
infrasound tapes was an excuse for not working—for not
being able to work. He hadn't written an original note of
music since Final Decision two years ago.

Mercifully, Jonathan's voice boomed through his
thoughts. "She blows, David. She blows."

Chapter 3

It was after hours. Colonel Gunnar Holst relaxed in the Common Room of the GF Satellite, which hung in stable orbit at LeGrange Point 5. He sipped a beer. It was from the latest batch, and it was colder than he liked.

He sipped the beer, warming it in his hands, and watched the latest three-vee drama unfold. He ignored the striking beauty of the full Earth outside the curving viewport of the Common Room. The sight failed to stir him anymore, unless he had had too much to drink and was feeling nostalgic. He had been a member of the elite Guardian Force for nearly thirty years now, and there were few new scenic wonders left for him to contemplate from that curving piece of glass.

Not that he was a contemplative man. His view could be stated in just a few words: Might Makes Right, and Orders Over All. His orders, when they came, would come from Earth. His superiors were the combined Ministry of WorldCo. Only the combined Ministry had the authority to order the unleashing of the L-5 warheads by the Guardian Force. In the meantime he waited and held the high ground.

He ran a free hand over his bullet head and clutched the beer with the other. The drama was a series they had been getting from Vesta. He watched as the little three-dimensional figures played out their roles. It was a story about a group of brave people who had colonized a distant planet and were victimized by a ruthless and corrupt Federation. One of the leading characters had had to make his choice between his adopted home or being a puppet of the government.

The little holo figure stood bravely before the depraved Federation man. He knew he was going to die, and he faced it bravely saying, "It is a far, far better thing I do than I have ever done before . . ." A tiny flash of a deadly smazer, then a sizzling sound, and the little man was gone.

Holst nodded approvingly. A show like that made a man think. He wondered what it would be like to die for an ideal. Somehow he knew that to die for freedom, like the man in the story, would bring eternal rewards. Cosmic rewards. A better life, he thought. Reward.

Freedom.

Suddenly, he realized that he valued freedom above all else. He nodded again at this revelation and sipped his warming beer. And as he sipped, he ran his fingers thoughtfully over the heavy silver T that hung at his throat.

Chapter 4

David was dozing in his skiptor compartment when the signal came on—time to engage webbing for the landing on Vesta. Groggily, he pulled the lever. Gossamer-light strands enveloped him.

The visiscreen showed the rocky curve of the asteroid set in the black of space. Stars blazed beyond Vesta's horizon.

He had been dreaming mixed fragmented dreams. They clung to him like mist. It had been seven years since he'd been put on the skiptor for earth. That time, Liss rode in a neighboring compartment; her face had been a constant companion on the little screen. In his dream, she looked the same— a freckled, blue-eyed child, but she was somehow an almost-adult too. Going back to Vesta for the ceremonies.

He shook his head, clearing it, and reached out for the drinking tube in the wall to his right. It slid out and he sucked deeply on it. The last hope of the dream fell away. Liss wouldn't be here. She was born on Hoffmeir; she'd join the Society of Adults there.

He'd never seen Hoffmeir. All he knew about it was what Liss had told him—that it was a man-made habitat with an artist's colony, a university, and a collection of government officials. He tried to invent from this a vision of Liss's home, but no pictures came to mind.

On his screen, the giant bays of Vesta were opening. He was really going home. He didn't know how to feel, so he settled on a place between scared and nervous. Today, he was

David Defour; tomorrow, he was going to meet his parents. Tomorrow, he was going to be somebody.

People gave him curious stares when he debarked and rode the zontilator toward the Arrow boarding area.

He wore the clothes of an Earther. The hood of his outer shirt was flung back revealing its lining, the rose-pink of music. The shirt felt warm in the controlled air of Vesta.

He adjusted the shoulder pack he carried. It felt light; he felt light—light as a duck feather. His muscles, strengthened by the pull of earth, could send him sailing over the crowd of people in a giant leap, he was sure. He looked from face to face, hoping for a familiar one. They were all strangers. Two minutes more, and he was boarding the sector six Arrow.

The Arrow pulled away from its boarding dock, gathered speed and surged along a tunnel until it burst out in the Dayglow of Periphery. Housing clusters squatted between clumps of greenery. In a minute, the Arrow sped by Dome Lake Park. The waters reflected the blue of the curving dome above it.

He had planned to head straight back to his old dorm, but instead, he got off at Arrow Hub and took the sublif to Sustenance Level.

He emerged to a Dayglow field of grain. Robotenders swung along the rows, tilling blades whirling.

David began to walk. It felt so strange to be back. It was as if his body and his mind were totally out of tune with Vesta. He reached in his pack and brought out his little recorder.

The needle swung into life in the audible range. It was picking up the faint hum of machinery—the mechanical pulse of Vesta. He turned a dial. Different sensors took over. He watched the tracings—the infrasound of Vesta itself, sub-audible sounds of molecule upon molecule of rock expanding and contracting. It was rhythmic, slow and totally unlike any earth tracing he'd seen.

He started to transpose the tracing into the audible range, but as he touched the dial, a fat drop of water struck his nose, followed by another smacking into his eye. In seconds he'd be caught in a downpour; it was a programmed shower. Running, head down, he scurried back to the sublif, jumped aboard and headed back to Arrow Hub.

"Name, please," said the woman. She wore the green uniform of Adolescent Center Dormitory.

He didn't know her. "David Defour."

She punched a code. Then she nodded, "Seven twenty-two." She handed him a slip of plaper embossed with his number.

Holding it, he stood confused for a minute. He'd forgotten his way. He looked around the wide room. Which way was corridor seven? Nothing looked familiar. Then he spotted it, walked down the long hall to the area marked "twenty-forty," and went in.

He'd never lived in this part before; he'd stayed in the level just below. He stood in a large commons room. One wall glowed green, while the three-dimensional words WEL-COME ADULTS emerged in cobalt blue. A large vinifountain spouted in the center of the room. Seven or eight boys his age stood around it, filling their cups from its straw-colored cascades. A dozen lounged on softies talking or watching the three-vee parade of younger children who marched along the main esplanade with festival banners.

Clutching his pack, he stood at the door and looked for someone he knew. Then hesitantly, he walked to the vinifountain, filled a cup, and slowly looked around the room.

"Who's that?" said one.

"Where?" asked another.

Only the sounds of the splashing fountain and the three-vee parade kept on as every voice hushed and every pair of eyes in the room stared at him.

"It's a mort," said a voice.

"Is it David?"

"It's David," said a red-haired boy.

Someone jostled his elbow. His cup sloshed and sent a little river down its side and onto the floor. He took a quick gulp and drained the glass.

They all began to speak at once: "He doesn't look so different from us."

"Not yet."

"Except for his clothes."

"Say, look at his ring."

"What's he wearing pink for?"

He stood staring at them. He felt his head begin to spin. Whether it was due to the drink or the crowd of people around him, he wasn't sure.

Then a blond boy said, "Leave him alone for a while, will you?" The crowd fell back and began to disperse. The boy took him by the arm saying, "What's your number?"

"Twenty-two."

They walked out of the commons into a hallway and came to another room. Five beds were rolled along the wall. "You're here," said the boy. "I'm over there. Do you remember me? I'm Martin."

Memories of a chubby boy snoring in the next bed came swirling back. They had been friends, but it was so long ago. What was the best way to take up the threads of a boyhood friendship? He wasn't sure, but he was happy to try.

He grinned. "Yes, I remember you." He thrust out his hand to Martin.

The boy stared at David's hand and made no move to take it for a few seconds. Then, he reached out stiffly and grasped David's. "I'm monitor here. I'll see to it that everybody leaves you alone."

David's grin slowly faded. "I thought maybe we could talk."

The boy withdrew his hand. "Oh. Well, that might be nice. But, right now, I'm busy." Martin turned away, paused, then said, "Let me know if anyone bothers you. If there's any trouble, I'm responsible." The boy stared at him for a moment, turned, and walked out of the room.

David sat still for a few minutes trying to understand what was happening. Then he got up and went back to the commons room. Martin stood near the fountain with a group of boys.

As David walked in, they stopped talking and stared at him curiously.

He looked at them one at a time, remembering. These were the boys he'd spent the first eleven years of his life with. They'd gone to school together, slept together, eaten together for the biggest part of their life. Standing near the fountain was Jeremy—red-headed, pale-skinned Jeremy. They'd driven fat Mother Chin crazy with their mischief. There, slumped on a softie near the wall, was Michael, pudgy and a little thick-headed, but always a friend. He'd helped Michael with his math nearly every night. He looked from one to the other as a thousand memories jostled in his brain, and then he said, "It was nice to see you all again, one last time."

As they stared, he shouldered his pack and walked out.

He didn't know where he was going, he only knew that he wanted to get away from there—from them.

He emerged briefly from a jumble of thoughts to find himself on the Arrow, headed for the main esplanade. The hurt splashed over him again. They'd made him feel like a malformed thing that belonged in a biologist's jar. Who did they think they were anyway? Bunch of technicians.

The Arrow sighed to a stop amid the glittering lights of Vesta's heart. He got off and stepped onto the zontilator. It carried him along the publicway, past the arena, past the concert hall and into an area of restaurants, shops and bars. He stepped off the zont onto the stationary walkway at its edge. For a while, he walked along it, feeling numb and very alone.

A flashing sign above a door caught his eye: "The Rings." He walked inside.

It was dark. Holos of the outer planets hung just above eye-level; their rings revolved slowly in translucent orbit. He found a seat near the door in a small pod. At the pressure of his body against the seat, a small communicator bank presented. A voice said, "How may we serve you?"

He wasn't hungry at all. He thought a moment, "Wine. I want a glass of wine." It seemed as good a way as any to spend the evening.

"Certainly." A choice list presented.

The list didn't mean anything to him. He pressed one at random.

"Credit, please."

He felt panicky for a moment; he didn't have a card. Then, he remembered and pressed his ring against the credex panel. A quick blue flash, then, in a moment, a small door slid open. He reached in, took out his glass of wine and began to sip. He barely noticed when the man and the woman came up to his side.

"We saw your little transaction," she said.

He looked up, puzzled.

"Your ring." She slid into the seat next to him. "Mind if we join you?"

"I guess not." He was a little confused by their attention.

"I'm Mria," said the woman. She was very pretty. Her hair was long and pale. As she leaned toward him, a strand of it fell across his hand.

"You're just off the skip, aren't you?" said the man. He was slim with curly dark hair.

David nodded.

"I knew it," the man said. He reached out and touched David's shoulder, squeezing softly. "My name is Ric. And what's yours?"

David's dark eyes flitted from one to the other. "David. My name's David."

"Here for the big day tomorrow?" Ric's hand stayed on his shoulder.

David nodded.

"We thought so," said Mria. Her hand fell lightly on his. She touched his ring, shivered once, and pressed her bare arm and shoulder against him.

She smelled wonderful. It had been a long time since a girl had touched him like that. He smiled at her shyly.

She looked deep into his eyes, and he looked back. Her eyes were pale and green. "You're pretty," he blurted.

She tilted her head coyly. One corner of her lips rose in a smile. "You've very sweet, David." Her fingers moved and twined through his. He felt a throbbing in his groin. He didn't know what was happening, but it was very pleasant. And she smelled so good.

Ric's hand began to knead his shoulder. "Tell me, David. How do you like us here?"

"Fine," he stammered.

Ric moved closer toward him and dropped his other hand to David's leg. The fingers played along his thigh.

He felt himself grow tense. The hand moved along his leg, massaging its way toward his groin. He pulled his body away from Ric and found it colliding with Mria's. A hot blush colored his face. "Stop it," he said.

The hand paused, moved again.

"Stop it, please."

"Leave him alone, Ric," said Mria. "He doesn't like you. He doesn't like men."

The hand stopped, pinched viciously, and was gone. Ric stood up, glaring at him. "Better think twice, little mort. You won't be pretty for long." With a final glare, he turned and walked out.

"I'm sorry for that," said Mria. "Ric is a little obnoxious at times."

Immensely relieved that the man had gone, David leaned back in his seat and breathed deeply. He was still blushing. He didn't know what to say to her. "Do you—Do you want some wine or something?"

"That would be wonderful, David." Her hair brushed across his cheek.

He ordered two drinks. He was beginning to feel a little giddy, a little drowsy.

She sipped hers and leaned closer toward him. He felt the length of her thigh press against his. His groin throbbed. "Why did you sit over here? With me?"

"You excite me, David." Her fingers began to explore his earlobe.

"I do?" His ear felt warm. Probably red like the rest of his face. He took a gulp of wine.

"You're so fresh. Like a flower. Something to be picked before it fades." She touched his neck. "They fade so quickly."

Slowly, realization dawned on him. "It's because I'm mortal. That's why you're—why I excite you."

"You do understand." Her fingers ran up into his hair, prickling the back of his neck. "The others, like me—they're always around. Whenever you want them. But you—"

He felt sick. He felt his body stiffen, and he felt sick. He

pulled himself away from her, staring at her all the while with
wide, dark eyes. Then he stood, throwing his pack over his
shoulder. He said, "I have to go now," and he was gone, out
the door, running down the walkway as if demons were after
him.

He got off the zont at the first place to stay he saw, the
State Hotel. The lobby was empty. He requested a room from
the communicator and pressed his ring against the credex
panel. A display flashed on the screen telling him where to go,
giving him his combination number. In a few minutes he
found his room, pressed the combo and locked the door behind him.

He set his pack on the floor and examined the bed lever.
It was an unfamiliar type, but the catch gave way with a
touch, and he sank down on the bed almost before it unrolled.
He felt exhausted.

He lay on his back for perhaps ten minutes staring at the
rosy ceiling panel, trying not to think about the things that
crowded into his mind. Twice today he'd felt like a freak—a
foolish, miserable freak—like something that normal people
look away from or else stare at to satisfy their curiosity.

The thoughts wouldn't go away. No matter how he tried
to divert himself, they kept creeping back, growing, jostling
his mind. After a few more minutes, he sat up and reached
for his pack. Opening it, he drew out his flute, and as he did
a half-dozen silver tapes spilled out. He looked at them ruefully, remembering his encounter with the whale man. He'd
been gathering his material for two years, his marvelous infrasound. He'd been using the tapes as substitutes for working—
but not anymore. Brushing them aside, he fitted his flute together. He'd take those thoughts that cluttered his mind,
those emotions that tore at his brain, and he'd push them out
of his flute. He could transform them, exorcise them.

He had a brief notion of the effect the piece he'd write
would have. They might look at him now like a strange creature from outer space or something, but they wouldn't for
long. They'd be too busy trying to get tickets to his concerts
and asking for his autograph on their programs.

He began to blow softly on his flute. The breathy notes rose and fell in an effortless scale and then in a series of arpeggios. He needed to warm up a bit, he told himself, then he'd let the ideas flow. As he played his scales, his exercises, the nagging thought came that he wasn't warming up for a concert, he was trying to write music. Wasn't he? Well, if that were so, then why was he exercising his fingers instead of his mind? And how could he warm up his mind?

He concentrated harder on the music he wanted to write. He flung the flute down on the bed and paced around the room, humming snatches of melody, rejecting them as derivative, or worse, ordinary.

Tomorrow would be better, he thought at last. Tomorrow he'd meet his parents. He'd belong somewhere. But then he had to ask himself, "and after that, what?" He was a mortal now. Sooner or later he'd have to pull away from his parents' world. He'd have to create—have to. It was all he had left now.

He sat on the bed again and lifted his flute to his lips. For an hour he played scales and arpeggios effortlessly, with the skill that came of long practice. And all the while, the tears streamed down his face.

He couldn't remember at first where he was. He rolled over, stared at the room, rubbed the sleep from his eyes and stared again. Gradually, he remembered—the hotel. At the door, the lock light still glowed.

He sprayed clean and pulled his clothes from the Ultrason, pleased that they felt fresh again. Fresher than he did, he thought as he picked up his pack and left the hotel. Outside, on the esplanade, he stepped on the zont and headed for the arena. Traffic was heavy. It looked as if everyone on Vesta was headed there too.

Banners fluttered in the vent streams as he rolled by. Near the arena, a uniformed group of twelve-year-old girls marched in formation, twirling shields that glittered bright in the Dayglow. One girl dropped hers. It spun in a silvery arc overhead until it dropped within reach of one of the dorm parents. Grinning, he flipped it back to the blushing girl.

At the gates of the arena, more banners fluttered, and he

could hear a band playing inside. The woman who seemed to
be in charge looked at his embossed plaper and said, "Check
your pack here, please."

He pulled it off his shoulder and handed it to her.

"Second lifter," she said, "then right."

He found himself just outside a door leading to the center
atrium of the arena. A woman in a green uniform paused in
her terse instructions to the group to glare at him for his
lateness. He stuck the badge she gave him onto his shirt and
self-consciously fell in with the group. In another minute, the
doors swung open and they marched into the arena. Although
there were no more than ninety eighteen-year-olds with him,
the arena was packed. He'd never seen so many people in one
place before.

An orchestra played the Song of Allegiance. Then suddenly a group of children ran across the field in front of David
—a somehow familiar group of children. He wrinkled his forehead in puzzlement. Why were they there? And why did they
seem familiar? Abruptly, he grinned. He knew why. He was
looking at himself and the rest of the troupe—holos of his
childhood.

The stream of children dissolved. Then the formal introductions began. A holo appeared of a baby in a tiny crib.
"Ginna Ayfour," said a voice. The crowd rustled its applause.

The list went on. At each name, an infant holo appeared.
When the voice called out, "David Defour," he was appalled
at the squalling red thing that projected. He felt relieved when
Janna Deseven's infant self took his place.

The parade of holos continued through the long ceremony. He saw himself as a toddler, a puny six-year-old and a
leggy ten-year-old. He wondered how his parents were react-
ing to these sights of him. They'd be given a commemorative
series of holos—one of each age. He grimaced. Maybe they
wouldn't want the one of him as a baby.

At a signal from the orchestra, a group of young girls ran
into the arena—real girls, he decided, not holos. They wore
the color code he'd worn when he first left Vesta—light blue,
so they were ten to twelve years old. They had been trained
for the dance.

As the music started, they began a series of gymnastic

moves that were different from the earth dances he'd seen. Then he realized why. The light gravity of Vesta made the difference—soaring aerial turns that would have been impossible on earth.

They were quite competent really, probably trained since they were four or five years old; but one girl was different.

She danced quite close to David. Tiny and lovely, her delicate heart-shaped face tilted away from the curve of her arm as she moved to the music. Her eyes were deep gray and turned upward at the edges, serious as they looked out toward the audience, but her mouth curved in a smile.

He couldn't stop watching her. When she danced, she floated, swam, soared, flew. When it was over, when the girls ran off the field, he felt a sense of loss and he couldn't imagine why.

Other dancers, singers and aerialists followed. Then the orchestra began the moving chords of "Our New Adults." The field, transformed at the hands of a visiographer, bloomed with roses—not as subtle as Lindner's work, but effective.

As the sounds of the orchestra faded, a voice said, "Ginna Ayfour, your parents welcome you." The girl stood and walked shyly to the center of the arena. From one side came a man and woman walking toward her. "The Honorable Cayse Rabb, the citizeness Lee Dana Rabb."

The couple walked up to the girl. They spoke, but David couldn't make out what they said, then all three were touching hands, then kissing and hugging.

His dark eyes glowed, yet he felt as if his insides were quivering. He knew his parents would be important people. They had to be; no one else, except mortals, was allowed to reproduce.

The voice said, "Congratulations, Ginna Rabb," and the girl walked slowly back to his group. Later, she would meet her parents again at the dinners and festivities that followed. That was when the parents introduced their new son or daughter to their circle of friends.

As each name was called, David grew more nervous. Finally, he heard his own. He walked to the center and looked anxiously toward the group of parents. A couple emerged and began to walk toward him

"The Honorable Ivan Trofimoff, and First Citizeness
Ruth Stine Trofimoff."

They were halfway to him now. Trofimoff, he thought.
That was his name. He sounded it softly, "Tro—feem—off,
David Trofimoff." Then they were there, the tall, thin man,
the small dark woman. They looked no more than twenty-five
or so.

"Hello," he said smiling shyly.

The woman came close. She was speaking, ". . . so sorry,
David, that we couldn't attend . . ." Her eyes weren't focused
on him, but on some place beyond him. ". . . so busy . . ."

He felt the shock slip over him as cold as the icy mountain
waters of Renascence. Holos. They were nothing but holos.
He could see the shimmery telltale signs around the edges of
the projections now.

The man was saying, ". . . trip was necessary . . ."

The woman said, ". . . must come for a visit sometime . . ."

Waves of pain and helpless rage washed over him. He
turned and walked back to the group, hoping no one noticed
him. He barely heard the rest of the ceremony. One thought
kept going through his mind—Trofimoff. He'd never use it;
he'd never take that name.

When the ceremony was over, the surge of the jostling
crowd swept him out of the arena. He reclaimed his pack from
the woman in charge and walked out onto the esplanade.

Long tables full of food lined the publicway. Everywhere
he looked, David saw people from his group with their new
parents, talking, eating, drinking from the vinifountains that
danced in the Dayglow.

He passed the food, the fountains, feeling his face burn
hot with embarrassment. He'd never take their name. He
stepped on the zontilator and didn't look back until the sounds
of the festival had faded to nothing. Then he allowed himself
to turn, to look wistfully over his shoulder. In another minute,
he'd reached the Arrow.

He got off the Arrow at skiptor boarding. He could only
think of one thing—Liss. He wanted to see Liss.

There was a skip leaving for Hoffmeir in two hours. When

it was his turn to board, the uniformed flightman looked at the badge on David's shirt and said, "You're missing the big day."

Hoffmeir had only a fraction of the population of Vesta. Thirty thousand people lived there, nine hundred of them mortals. It was the largest colony of artists and musicians in the belt.

David was bewildered as he looked around. He'd never been in an artificial habitat before. He stood near the periphery and looked around in awe. You could see it all from one place! Across the area where clustered dwellings were interspersed with low green shrubs, he could see a round green belt and then, beyond, more housing.

He seemed to be looking down in a basin, but when he whirled around, it was he that stood in the bowl. Hills, dotted with structures, rose around him. He was briefly dizzy.

There was no Arrow here, only a network of moving zontilators. He found a communicator bank and asked for Liss McNabb.

The machine voice said, "Information not available."

He didn't know what to do; then he thought of calling her parents. Within a minute, a woman's voice said, "Cara, here." The visiscreen came into focus. She was a middle-aged version of Liss. Her blue eyes stared at him.

For a moment he couldn't speak, and then he said, "I'm David. David Defour, from Renascence. I'm looking for Liss."

A smile came warmly over the screen. "Oh, yes. Liss told us about you. How nice that you're here. But Liss and Kurt have gone to Earth. She'll be so sorry she missed you."

"Liss and Kurt?"

The woman paused. "Oh, didn't you know? They entered a term-contract of marriage shortly after she left Renascence."

The words didn't register for a few moments. "A term-contract?" But that was never issued unless the people had permission to have a child. "A term-contract?" he said again. His voice sounded strange to him. "With Kurt?"

"Yes. Kurt Kraus. He's the Minister of Culture."

The image of the man at Tanya Rolfe's funeral came rushing back. He stood staring helplessly at the screen.

"Their baby is at Cluster Dorm," said the woman. "We wanted to keep her with us, but it wasn't allowed." She sighed, then she said, "She's fifteen months old now."

Somehow he managed to say his goodbyes to Liss's mother. Somehow he managed to draw breath into his lungs and modulate it out again in syllables and words.

When the screen went blank, he continued to stare at it for a while as if it were of extreme interest. Then he began to walk.

He found himself on a zontilator. He didn't know where it was going, but it didn't matter. After a while, he heard music. He looked dully around. It was an artist's colony. A collection of boys and girls were dancing on a little patch of green to the music of a trio of woodwinds—a rehearsal of some sort. An old man sat with a plastique board across his lap making deft impressions of the dancers with his stylus.

Without realizing it, David stepped off the zont. The old man reached for a bottle and sprayed a thin film over the plastique. As David watched, the clear fluid changed to opaque buff. The old man peeled the picture from the plastique and looked at it. The bronzed lines of the sketch stood in stark relief from the pale film. As the film moved in the old man's hands, the figures seemed to dance.

The artist smiled up at David. His skin was translucent from extreme age; his cheeks were pink. "How can I help you, son? Are you lost?"

David looked at him, and then without knowing why, he said, "I'm looking for Cluster Dorm."

"Why, it's right over there." David's gaze followed the bent old finger. It pointed at a large structure beyond a small pond with a central fountain. The dorm was about a tenth of a kilometer away.

"Thank you," he said, but he made no move to go.

"You're from earth," said the old man. "Renascence." His fingers moved, smoothing the plastique.

David nodded.

"You wear the colors of music." Gnarled fingers guided the stylus over the sketchboard. "What do you play?"

"Cythar and flute—and the symphosizer. I use it to compose. I—I'm a composer." He watched the old man's hands; he couldn't meet his eyes. He'd barely been able to get the words out. Composer. Lie. Anxiously, he looked at the old artist. Did he know?

The old man reached for his bottle and sprayed a layer of liquid over the plastique. As the film grew opaque, he watched David keenly. "It's hard for many of us at times—at first." He peeled the film from the picture, looked at it and handed it to David.

It was a quick sketch, only a few lines, but it had captured David's expression.

"Keep it, son," said the old man. "Maybe you'll need to look at it one day."

David muttered his thanks and turned away, glancing at the picture again. He found it disturbing. It was the eyes: wide, dark and, somehow, very remote.

He told the woman in charge of Cluster Dorm, "I want to see Liss Kraus's baby."

The bored look on her face faded. "You do? We don't have many requests to see the children." She checked the communicator and then said, "Follow me."

He walked with her down a corridor, wondering the whole time why he was there. It was as if he had to come, had to prove to himself that Liss was really gone forever. At the end of the corridor, another hallway intersected, and they turned left. They stopped outside a wide curtained window.

The woman pressed a button in the wall. When someone answered, she said, "Visitor to see Alani Elten."

"Right away."

"They'll open the curtain in a moment," she told David, "then you can look in."

"I want to go inside," he said. He didn't know why he said it.

"Oh, no. It isn't allowed."

"Why not? I want to go in."

She seemed shocked. "It's never allowed. If we permitted intermingling, then the ones who aren't allowed to reproduce would be jealous. We can't have discontent," She stared at him. "It's against all the rules."

The curtain opened, and David looked through the one-way window into the nursery. There were seven toddlers in the room and two dorm Mothers. One of them said, "Come here, Alani." As David watched, a tiny girl took two tottery steps toward the Mother, and then started to fall. She saved her balance by planting two pudgy hands on the floor. She wobbled like that for a moment or two with her little bottom sticking up in the air. Then the baby managed to stand up and take two more steps before her balance gave way entirely and she plopped abruptly to her diapered rear with a surprised look on her face.

The dorm Mother swooped down on the child with a laugh. Picking her up, the woman planted a kiss on a fat little cheek and brought her to the window.

David blinked. The baby looked like Liss. She peered out of clear blue eyes, and her nose was a tiny pug. And she was wearing something around her neck—a little gold chain with a small amethyst dangling from it.

He drew in a breath. Liss hadn't even kept the necklace; she'd put it around the neck of her baby—Kurt Kraus's baby.

He turned away from the window. So it really was over. He'd never see Liss again. He muttered his thanks to the woman in charge and walked out of Cluster Dorm, feeling more alone than he had ever felt before.

The next day, he caught the first skiptor back to earth. It was a hopper with a stop at Vesta on the way.

After stowing his pack in the saf-T-cab of the compartment and settling back in his seat, he switched on the music bank and tried not to think; but his mind slipped into freefall long before the skiptor did.

What was he going to do now? He was running away, he knew, but he didn't fit anymore—not in Vesta—not on Hoffmeir either. So he was running back to Renascence. On the surface of it, the thought gave him comfort. It would be good to be back, to feel the cool air, see the shadows on the mountains—but then what? What was he going to do with the rest of his life? If he couldn't work, couldn't compose. . . . He wouldn't fit there either.

The thought settled coldly in his head. It was true. He didn't belong at Renascence—not any more than Liss did—but she'd had sense enough to know it. He didn't belong at Renascence, and now, he didn't belong anywhere else either.

The coldness spread, chilling him. His fingers curled, making fists. He felt nails bite into his palm, and he squeezed his hands tighter, hanging onto the pain in them, hanging onto it because the other pain was harder to bear.

The white skin stretched over his knuckles. Slowly he opened his hands, staring at them, at the ring he wore. It glowed dully in the diffused cabin light. If he'd never put it on, his music would have died naturally. And wouldn't that have been better? Better than to let it erode his soul a bit at a time until there was nothing left.

He felt hot tears sting his eyes. He was a drone—a bum. Like the whale man. Fit for nothing more than to wander alone over the earth without even a dream—without even the hope of one.

The skiptor had a short layover in Vesta, then once again the huge bays opened, and the ship moved into the black vacuum of space.

David switched off the music bank and sat in silence in his compartment staring at the visiscreen with its thousands of stars; but the images didn't register on his brain.

He'd eaten nothing since the day before; he felt no hunger now. He felt nothing at all except for a pervasive numbness, a remoteness. Finally, he became aware of the screen in front of him full of points of light, isolated, just as he was.

When the face came on the screen, speaking to him, it was an intrusion and he didn't want to hear the words.

". . . hesitated to invade your privacy, but I knew you were from Renascence . . . " It was the flightman. ". . . this child is near hysteria . . . would you help? She's in cabin six."

David blinked. He was supposed to help someone?

"If you would, just flip on your intercom," said the flight-man. "Compartment six."

He looked at the man's face on the screen for a moment, then he said, "Why not?"

The flightman thanked him, and the face disappeared. David reached out and pressed the button for compartment six.

A view of the compartment flashed on the screen. Dwarfed by the seat she huddled in, a girl sat curled in a ball of misery, hands pressed over her face, knees drawn up to her chest. She seemed to be choking. Sharp gasps shook her thin little body. Pale hair fell over tear-wet fingers.

Alarmed, David said, "Hello." And then immediately felt like a fool. But what else could he say? He didn't even know her name.

She didn't respond to his voice—just kept making those terrible gasping moans. She wore the light blue uniform of the ten- to twelve-year-olds of Vesta Central.

Obviously she'd been taken aboard that morning with only the sketchiest notion of where she was going or why. In a shivering instant, he was eleven years old again and terrified —going to a place called Renascence, exiled from the only home he'd ever known. "Stop it," he said. "Don't cry."

The sharpness of his voice startled her; she looked up. Her face was red and swollen from crying, but not enough to disguise its delicate heart-shaped lines. Wet gray eyes tilting upward at the edges peered at him.

He stared back with a shock of recognition. It was the little dancer he'd seen at the Ceremony of Adults. "I know you," he said. "I saw you dance. What's your name?"

The gasping sobs continued, "St—St—Stoey," she managed to say and then buried her face in her hands again.

He knew her pain—he could feel it. It was like his own had been. He tried to divert her, "I guess you want to be a dancer. You'll make a wonderful dancer, Stoey."

The hand stayed clamped over her face. She shook her head, then was wracked by another series of sobbing gasps.

"Don't you want to be a dancer?"

She shook her head again. "A chor—A chor—A chor—e
—og—rapher."

Her misery communicated through the screen so well
that David felt his breath catch in rhythm with hers. He
wished he could reach out, touch her, pet her, comfort her.
Instead he said, "You'll like Renascence. You can learn to be
a fine choreographer there."

The sobbing started up again, harder. He'd said the
wrong thing to her. Couldn't he *ever* think of the right thing
to say? He tried again, "I lived in Renascence. A long time.
I'm going back."

She sucked in a hard breath and peeped at him between
her fingers. "You—You are?"

He nodded. "It's nice there. It really is. Renascence has
mountains and waterfalls and wild animals. And—the wind
blows."

The girl looked at him in horror, hands doubled in fists
against her face.

He'd done it again. He'd scared her more, instead of comforting her. How could he have been so stupid? He looked
around the compartment in despair. If only he could tear
through those walls that enclosed him—get to her somehow
—make her understand. Then, he had a thought. He pulled
open the cabinet and hauled out his pack. "I'll show you,
Stoey. It'll be all right."

He pulled out his recorder and a bright silver tape disc.
At that moment, the skiptor moved into freefall, and his cabin
was filled with a dozen silver discs floating through the air.

He slammed the pack shut, just as his flute began to
nudge its way out. Releasing his restraining harness, he
grabbed at the little tapes as they drifted by.

Stoey's eyes grew wide at his frantic activity. She forgot
to cry.

When the recalcitrant tapes were at last corralled, he
pulled down his pack from its perch near the ceiling, stowed
all but one tape back inside, and managed to slip that one into
his recorder. Then he pushed the machine under a restraining
strap and turned it on, twirling a dial, bringing the infrasound
up to just audible range. "Listen, Stoey. Listen," he said ur-

gently. "This is Renascence. This is the song the Earth sings. Listen."

The slow, low-pitched familiar rhythms of Renascence began to play. Stoey's eyes grew even wider. "It's—heavy there," she managed to say.

"But that isn't all, Stoey. Renascence has bird songs and little creek sounds. It—" He clenched his fist once in his attempt to make her understand. Then he drew his pack to him and carefully pulled out his flute. "Listen, Stoey. It's like this."

Against the slow insistent infrasound rhythms, he blew a soft bird call into his flute—the call of a wood thrush throbbing its sweet sad notes in a damp wood. *Ee—o—lee, Ee—o—lay, Ee—o—lee.* It ended in a trill. He blew another wood thrush—answering, inventing. The trill ended in the rush of a tiny stream chattering, laughing, dancing from rock to rock.

Stoey looked at him with something more than tears shining from her gray eyes. He felt elated; he was making her understand. He blew again into his flute, and the music that came out whispered like new poplar leaves. He blew the erratic whimsical rhythms of a hopping rabbit, a fragile fawn.

Out of the corner of his eye, he watched the screen. He saw Stoey reach down and release the restraining harness that bound her until she floated free at the end of a single tether. She began to dance.

She danced so subtly, so beautifully that she took his breath from him. Then he found it again and blew into his horn, matching the flute sounds to the movements of her body.

He marveled at it. There in the cramped confines of her little compartment, she moved to the music like a fragile bird in a cage. He varied rhythms, tried to fool her body with them, but she danced as if she were a thought that moved within his mind.

And neither he nor Stoey stopped until the tape—the song of Renascence—came to an end.

They boarded the Renascence hover at Biscayne-Atlantic Terminal and talked until the mountains came into view. Then they watched through the curving windows as the hover swooped along the rushing river. When the clearing came in sight, the craft's forward motion slowed, and it settled gently to the ground.

He helped her out of the hover, watching her face, seeing her take her first look at Renascence.

She managed a little smile, but it vanished as her knees buckled from the unaccustomed pull of Earth's gravity. "Oh, I'll never be able to dance here."

He caught her arm, steadying her, "Yes, you will. It'll make you stronger."

She looked around her again at the green clearing and the smoky blue mountains beyond. Her gray eyes were huge and luminous, "You were right, David. It feels like you told me it would."

He smiled down at her, not contradicting her, not wanting to, because he *had* told her—with his music. Then, he suddenly knew what music really was—communication. Strange that he'd never realized it before. He'd cut it off and then called himself lonely. Even a whale would know better. Even a whale.

He grinned. He was eighteen now; he was a man—a man who could learn to be as smart as a whale. He felt himself grin wider, idiotically, but he didn't mind at all.

He guided the little girl with wobbling legs toward a small wooden cabin next to the lake. "Come on, Stoey. First you need to rest awhile," he said, "and then I'll show you what home looks like."

Chapter 5

In the dark of the moon, a thousand stars glittered over Renascence. A breeze tangled in the new leaves. The creek spun foam and drummed its waters in a rocky hollow outside David's cabin. The light from his window winked with his passing as he walked back and forth in front of the single lamp.

While all Renascence slept, he paced, then dropped to a hunching seat before his console, then rose to pace again.

They had brought him dinner as they had every night for a month. It sat untouched on a small table against the wall.

A whippoorwill began to call in the darkness, and then another answered faintly in the distance. Finally David sat again before his console and did not leave his perch until the sun shone yellow over the mountains and glittered on the riffling waters of the lake.

The door to his cabin burst open then, and he ran out into the sunlight bearing a sheaf of print-outs from the symphosizer. He raised them in one hand held high over his head and, with a whoop of exultation, shook them at the world.

He jumped in the air, came down, touching toes just once on the little porch, and leaped to the ground, running as he touched—running, whooping, with madhouse glee.

He sprang along the edge of a tiny spring studded with pale green ferns and shaded by sycamore and oak. As if possessed, he leaped back and forth in an eccentric zigzagging path along the little stream, then veered off in a hopping gait through a daisy field, startling a rabbit in his path.

After pausing once to shake the print-outs once again in the face of the sun, he flipped himself in a somersaulting roll and came up balancing precariously on one foot.

Then leaping and shouting, he threw open the door to the dining hall, running among the people dawdling over a late breakfast, shaking his manuscript in their amazed faces. "It's good! It's really good!" And before they could recover their wits, he ran out again, whooping like a maniac. Along the lake shore he ran in and out of the water's edge, splashing, yelling to the mountains, "It's good!"

Two dozen startled faces watched his progress as he followed the curve of the lake toward the Common Hall, yelling, shaking his manuscript and pausing now and then to leap into the air.

A couple in a rowboat stared as he made his crazed progress around the lake, ran up the wide stone steps of the Common Hall and burst in, interrupting a mime show with a yell. "It's good! It is! It's good!" He flung his manuscript into the air. Ducking the fluttering rain of pages, the people inside stared at his amazing progress through the building and out on the wide cantilevered deck that overhung the lake. He scrambled up on the railing and, with a final screech of delight, launched himself, mouth open, into the bone-chilling waters.

He sank like a stone, emerged, sank again, and rose once more, yelling, choking, sputtering. "E-s-ss glood!" He gulped and sank again.

The rowboat pulled up in his wake and offered him the end of an oar. Grinning, sputtering, he grabbed it.

"I guess he's finished his masterpiece," said someone amid the laughing from the deck above. "I wonder what he'll call it?"

"No question," said another, " 'Music to Drown By.' "

Chapter 6

Dayglow on Hebe had faded to shades of gray on charcoal. The lights of Colony Park spread dim pools on the phalanx of marching children.

They drilled precisely, perfectly, to the muffled beat of drums. Lights spun hypnotically from their whirling shields.

Kurt watched from the reviewing stand. Liss sat next to him. For a time, she had entered notes in the small machine she held, but now she stared at the shields and the light patterns. There was a look on her face that disturbed Kurt. It was a look he had seen before, a look that comes into the eyes of people who ring disasters—first a shocked widening, as if the eyes must dilate to take in all the scene, and then, glittering excitement.

Her mouth was slightly open, her eyes locked on the whirling shields. He touched her hand. She ignored it, staring down at the marchers, and her lips began to move in concert with the drumbeat.

Kurt leaned toward her, "What is it, Liss?" He put his head near hers and strained to hear.

She stared ahead; her lips moved—a whisper, "Silver T . . . Silver T. . . ."

A man at the periphery of the crowd leaped to his feet. His amplified voice carried easily over the drumbeat, "Give us Commerce."

Kurt's eyes narrowed. The man was a plant. Part of an overall plan. Since the assassination of the Minister of Commerce, the colonies had organized to demand that Prime Minister Gerstein appoint a successor from the belt. And Deputy Minister Tarantino had smiled ingenuously and pointed out that indeed there had never been a minister from among the colonists. Perhaps now was the time to listen to the people. He spoke of the "face of resolution," intimating how difficult it was to change public opinion, shaking his head sadly as if he were not quite equal to the task. But he would, of course, cooperate with Earth in any way.

The plant in the audience yelled again, "Give us Commerce." The people echoed it, fitting it to the cadence of the muffled drums, the wheeling shields. "Commerce . . . Commerce . . . Commerce. . . ."

The children below drilled on, to a faster cadence now. They performed with a measured frenzy to the chant of thousands.

Kurt stared at the field. He was watching a masterful performance, a performance with all the spontaneity of a machine. And the performance was being broadcast to every colony in space.

He looked uneasily at Liss. She stared ahead. Her lips moved with the cadence. He took her hand.

Her hand clutched his; her voice rang with the others, "Commerce . . . Commerce . . . Commerce. . . ."

"Liss?"

She squeezed his hand, twisting his fingers cruelly, and began to pant, gasping as if she were suffocating.

"Liss!"

She turned her face to him then. Beads of sweat stood out on her forehead. Her brow was arched, her eyes wide with horror. She stared into his without seeing them, and to the cadence of the drums her lips moved again: "Awful, awful, awful, ohgod, awful. . . ."

He stood and, with an arm around her, lifted her to a standing position, half-walking, half-dragging her into a small dim room in the back. The people around them seemed oblivious as they chanted to the rhythm of the whirling shields.

"Help me," Kurt said to the Deputy Minister's aide who had followed him automatically.

The woman stared at him without seeming to understand.

"Help me with her," he snapped. "She's sick."

"Sick," repeated the aide blandly. And then as Kurt struggled with Liss and managed to lay her down on soft cushions,
the woman stared at the sobbing girl. Slowly comprehension
spread over her face. "Why she's sick," she said at last. She
leaned over Liss, touched her brow, looked with concern into
the girl's eyes. And as she did, the heavy silver T at her throat
swung and glittered in the flickering light.

Kurt stared at the communicator terminal and read the
bio-sketch again:

> TARANTINO, SILVIO ANTHONY: Born M-G 17,
> New Providence Island, Consolidated Bahamian
> Sector, Earth.
> Father: Victor Luis Tarantino, deceased M-G 29.
> Mother: Caterina "Kitty" Theresa Martez Tarantino,
> deceased M-G 57.
> Dormitory: Victoria, N.P. M-G 17–35.
> Studies: Acad. of the Azores M-G 35–39.
>   Spec. Studies WorldCo ComSchool M-G 39–
> 41. . . .

He narrowed his eyes intently and skimmed the lines: . . .
Spec. Studies WorldCo ComSchool. ComSchool.

Tarantino had been Vesta's Com Chief when they found
the altered records of the children. He remembered Mallory's
voice as the cryptist said, "The child's age was transposed with
the dorm number . . . cleverly crude . . . We can't prove it
was intentional. . . ."

Kurt spoke to the communicator: "Bio-sketch, Tarantino,
Victor Luis."

INSUFFICIENT DATA.

"Reenter: Tarantino, Victor Luis. Consolidated Bahamian Sector, Earth. Deceased M-G 29."

NO RECORD TARANTINO, VICTOR LUIS.

"Bio-sketch, Tarantino, Caterina "Kitty" Theresa Martez."

TARANTINO, CATERINA "KITTY" THERESA. . . .

"Complete bio."
As the communicator complied, Kurt blinked at the words:

. . . Subject, single.
Father: unknown
Mother: Tarantino, Clara Maria, deceased M-G 20.
　　　　Residence at death Tampa, Florida Sector,
　　　　Earth. Bay Hospital for the Mentally Aber-
　　　　rant.
TARANTINO, CATERINA "KITTY" THERESA:
Deceased M-G 1. Residence at death Tampa, Florida
Sector . . . (reg. suicide). . . .
Issue: 1 son(s) (reg. illegitimate) Tarantino, Silvio
Anthony, b. M-G 1. o daughter(s). . . .

Tampa. Tarantino hadn't been born in the Bahamas at all. He had altered his own records and given himself a father he had never had, a background he had never had. Born in Tampa—in the first year of the process. He would have been in protective custody at MacDill at the same time Kurt was.

He called for the MacDill records, but when they flashed across the screen, he suddenly realized that they were unnecessary as a memory from nearly two hundred years ago came back to life. . . .

He was twenty years old again, watching as the last of a dying sun glinted on the coppery hair of a limp figure on the stretcher.

"Sean? It looks like Sean."

. . . The other boy was dead; killed in the fire that blackened the little classroom. By some miracle, Sean was alive.

"Who did this to you, Sean?"

Tears rolled down the freckled face. "One of the little
kids, Kurt. He had a birthmark here," Sean pointed to the
angle of his jaw. "I don't know his name. He locked us in . . ."

. . . The girl laughed. "Kurt, are you seriously suggesting
a five-year-old could do something like this on purpose? . . ."

. . . The teacher stood and glared at Kurt. "Your accusation of this child was completely vicious and unconscionable."
She turned toward the little boy and wrapped her hands
around his shoulders. "Thank God, no one believed you." She
patted the child nervously, "It's all over, Silvio. You can forget
about this now."

Very calm, very quiet, the boy stood next to her. He
looked at Kurt for a long moment, and in that moment Kurt
saw something flicker beneath the artless baby veneer—something so old, so malevolent that he felt a sudden chill.

"I don't forget," Silvio said. "Ever." And then the look of
virgin innocence slid back again and a chubby thumb crept to
his lips. . . .

The cherub face of the Deputy Minister superimposed
itself on the memory of a five-year-old boy—a child whose
monstrous smile showed not a flicker of guilt or conscience.

"I don't think you fully understand what I'm saying."
Ready to catch the slightest nuance of expression, Kurt leveled his gaze at the Prime Minister.

"I understand that I'm being coerced," answered Gerstein. "You're asking me to appease the very people who murdered Minister Chavez. To the victor, the spoils."

"For a reason. The construction of the Ram has taken
me to the belt quite a lot lately. I've seen things there that
others may have missed. Remember, I was present the day of
Chavez's assassination, and I assure you that the manner of
his death was no accident."

Gerstein raised an eyebrow. "Obviously. No one doubts
that it was murder."

"Exactly. It was meant to be obvious. We were meant to
know that it was an act of defiance. And why? If someone
merely wanted Chavez dead, it would have been a simple

matter to arrange an accident, a clever cover-up instead of a blatant murder. The question is, who gains from all this?"

Gerstein took a slow sip of his brandy before he said, "Who does, Kurt?"

"Someone called Silver T." He paused and then told Gerstein about Liss, about her loss of memory and her reaction on Hebe. "I think Silver T is your Deputy Minister, Silvio Tarantino. I think he staged the murder of Chavez and then caused the colonists to agitate for the appointment of a new minister, knowing that you would refuse."

"For what reason?"

"To guarantee his complete control of the colonies. To finish the job of polarizing the people of the belt against Earth."

"To prime the revolutionary pump, so to speak," said Gerstein.

"Yes."

Gerstein stared at the brandy snifter he held. Setting it on the table, he ran his fingers over the smooth glass and stared at the liquid inside as if it were an augur, a crystal ball, that would give up its secrets if only he looked long enough. Finally he said, "You have no proof."

"No," he admitted.

"I had hoped you did. You aren't the first one to come to me with suspicions." Gerstein cleared his throat. "An accusation now, without proof, would accomplish just what he wants; a polarization of opinion—perhaps worse."

Kurt nodded.

"I can delay announcing the successor to Commerce for a while longer." Gerstein leaned back, tented his fingers and looked at Kurt. "We've known matters were growing worse in the belt. We've seen the spoor of the beast for quite a while. Now, while he stalks, we have to move just out of reach until we have him in a corner—a very quiet and unobtrusive corner." He looked at Kurt speculatively. "Everyone knows of your interest in the Ram. Your travel in the belt attracts less attention than the rest of us." He paused, as if trying to decide what to say.

"You want me to find proof," said Kurt.

Gerstein met his gaze, "You won't be working alone," he said, "but you don't need to know who the others are with one exception. I want you to contact the foreman of the Ram. His name is Jacoby."

"We've met."

Gerstein reached in a desk drawer and took out an antique silver dime. "Give him this."

Kurt turned it over in his hand.

"And be careful. I sent a man to L-5. I received word this morning of his death." Gerstein's voice was calm, almost too calm. "They assured me that it was an unfortunate accident."

The two men stared at each other. The thought went unsaid, but it hung in the air like a palpable thing: L-5, under the control of the Guardian Force, harbored the warheads of the system.

Jacoby swung off the Ram's central zont hub and spoke into a small microphone slung around his neck. "Rogers, get a team going on that electrolapse in Central Archives." He listened for a few seconds, then said, "And I want a crew in the dorm squatter." A pause. "You give it your best strain, Rogers, and then you'll know what's wrong." He added darkly, "Oh, will you know . . ."

Scowling impatiently, Jacoby listened again, "I don't give a long dark-brown if they are. Short or not, you get them there, quantum. And tell them to beam on my mark." He thumbed the microphone off and waved his slip-stick in Kurt's direction by way of greeting. "Glad to have you aboard, Citizen."

Kurt stepped off the zont and joined him. "What's that weapon you're carrying?" He indicated Jacoby's stick.

"My slip-stick?" Jacoby grinned. "The crews hate it. When I find a lapsus on the job, I touch it with my magic wand." He showed Kurt the end of it. "A dab of audio paste comes out here. It squawks into their com-sets when they get close. The more paste, the louder it gets. A superlapse gets more, and I really dump on a megalapse." He grinned and ran his hand down the slip-stick. "I call it my Ram rod. The crews have already told me what they plan to do with it when this job is over. Now, what can I do for you?"

Kurt smiled. "You can begin by showing me where my quarters will be."

Jacoby cocked his head as he looked at Kurt, "So you've decided to go with the Ram. Well, good grade. I'm glad to hear it. Is it still quiet?"

"Still quiet," said Kurt. "Nobody knows yet except you, me and Gerstein. Keep it that way for a while."

Jacob nodded. With a jerk of his head, he indicated a zont marker. "Each hemi is marked in quads," he said. "Your quarters will be in 3."

The two men stepped up and the zont began to move them among a series of buildings interspersed with young landscaping. Jacoby pointed to his right. "Over there is Communications. Most of Central Com is underground. Archives is next door. So is Education Central and Panmedia. I think I might like to do something in media when I retread."

Kurt looked at him thoughtfully.

Jacoby shot a sharp glance at Kurt. "We *will* retread, won't we? Just like we do now? I mean, I like the work I'm doing, but I can't see doing it forever."

"You can retrain for something else," said Kurt, "whenever you like. I was just wondering what I might want to retrain for some day."

A look of disbelief crossed over Jacoby's face. "A minister retrain? It's never happened."

"Maybe it's time it did."

"Here we are." Jacoby hopped off the zont. Kurt followed. They were about five hundred meters from the central courtyard hub. Now, they stood in a terraced garden. "The Prime Minister's office is central," said Jacoby. "Entertainment areas are to the left, living quarters, right."

The door was stuck. Jacoby struggled with it unsuccessfully for a moment, then opened it with bull force. Disgusted, he aimed his slip-stick and shot a blob of audio paste at the offender. After a sidelong look at Kurt, he deposited a second blob alongside the first. He triggered the stick and sprayed an activating coating over the two lumps. They'll hear that one," he said with satisfaction.

Inside, they stood in a central atrium. To the left, a pair of heavy doors opened into a series of large rooms for dining and entertainments, to the right was the private quarters entrance. At the rear of the atrium was a carved wooden door with the words PRIME MINISTER in relief. Kurt felt a pang at the sight of them. It seemed he had always been Kurt Kraus, Minister of Culture, and Gerstein had always been Prime Minister. The words emphasized the autonomy of the Ram and brought home to him, as nothing else had, how final her trip would be.

The door to the office slid open easily, and they stepped inside. The office was much like his own on Earth, furnished, but bare of personal effects. It gave Kurt a slightly eerie feeling. No paintings hung from the walls, no sculpture perched on his desk, no projections, no light poems. The room was silent, and Kurt realized with a start that there had never been music on the Ram. It was going to carry human beings and their culture to the stars, this silent silver egg, and music had never played here.

But it would, he resolved, and soon. He was going to fill the ship with the music he had known and loved. It was a way to remember. There could never be the change of seasons on the Ram, but there would be Copland's "Appalachian Spring" and Tanya Rolfe's "Summer Conserere." There would never be an ocean, or a chill wind, or a wild fawn on the Ram, and he was suddenly struck with this, with the almost unbearable nostalgia of it. And he realized then, how easy it would be for the people to forget.

He couldn't let them. He wouldn't let them forget Earth itself. He'd give them paintings of it, poetry of it, the new music of it that the boy, David Defour, had composed. He had not yet heard David's "Earth Song," but word of it had reached him. Something new, they said, something different in music, and yet at the same time, something very old and familiar—music from the very Earth itself. They had to remember, because human beings were made of memories. If they lost them, they would be less than what they were, less than what they could be.

As if reading his mind, Jacoby said, "It seems strange now, but after a while the Ram will be like home."

Kurt looked at him steadily for a moment, and then he said, "And what about what we leave behind—Earth and the colonies. What's going to happen there?"

"I told you I consider myself apolitical."

In answer, Kurt took out a thin silver dime. He flipped it on the table where it spun in slowing circles and finally fell still.

Jacoby picked it up, held it, turned it over. "Silver," he said, "it's an interesting subject. Silver is by nature the best conductor of heat and electricity—a conduit for power. People want it, crave it. They've even killed for it."

"Yes," said Kurt, "and they may again."

"He's got the people, you know," said Jacoby slowly. "He's got their minds. And they don't even know it."

"How can we fight him?"

Jacoby stared at him for a moment, then shook his head. "I wish I knew. They think he has special powers. And sometimes I wonder. Sometimes I think they may be right."

Kurt raised an eyebrow. "Powers?"

Jacoby nodded. "Something inside. Something ordinary people don't have. A way to manipulate people, read their thoughts, influence them. We know he's using the media for his purposes, but there's more to it than that."

"Are you saying you believe that Tarantino has some kind of occult power?"

"I don't know. I'm not sure what I believe. But I do know that the people of the belt believe it."

Kurt sat down at the oval conference table and stared at its polished surface for a few seconds before he said, "You're a rational man, Jacoby."

"And therefore I'm above believing in ghoulies and ghosties and flying saucers," said Jacoby. "You're right. But once in a while, one of us shows up who isn't quite one of us. I don't know what it is that's different, but the people sense it. And when they do, the power grows."

"You're talking about the powers of persuasion—charisma," said Kurt. "The power of a Hitler. It's human, Jacoby."

"Is it?" He stared at Kurt as if trying to read his face.

"These people will die for him if necessary. They believe by dying for him they'll be giving up their immortality for something infinitely better."

Kurt said, "You're saying that they think he's a messiah."

Jacoby said, "I wonder if he is."

Chapter 7

A breeze came down the mountain to Renascence, riffling the leaves of poplar and oak, casting a layer of sun-diamonds on the surface of the lake. It stole through the windows of the Common Hall and touched the hair of the eleven-year-old choreographer who worked at a console. "David, help me. I can't get it right."

He looked up from his position on the floor. He sat cross-legged among an array of records and tapes. "What's wrong, Stoey?"

"I can't get the enhancer to work."

Groaning, he untangled his long legs and got up. "What kind of effect are you after?" He looked at the staging area. Two tiny stylized figures moved in a pas de deux. "It looks fine to me."

"Da-vid!" Her voice colored with exasperation. "I've got a show to put on for the children. They'll need a magnifying glass for this."

Grinning, he turned a switch and twitched a dial. The figures grew to Brobdingnagian proportions, towering above them, so solid-looking that when the smaller of the two leaped, then flipped, Stoey ducked involuntarily, "Da-vid!"

Grinning wider, he cranked the figures down to human size, but this time they were blood-red, then abruptly blue. Stoey watched, tipping her small heart-shaped face in amazement, as the rainbow figures danced before her, now blue, now violet, now shades of pink shot with orange. "I like it. I really like it. And so will the children." She clasped her hands together. "They'll love it! Now, quick. Shut it off before they get here."

He clicked the console off, and the figures disappeared.

"Are you sure you know how to do that again?" she asked doubtfully. "I mean, with the colors and everything?"

David nodded and said with mock gravity, "I think I can manage it."

They heard voices, and then the wide doors opened. Led by two teachers, a dozen children between the ages of five and ten came in. They had slanted eyes with puffy lids; their hair was coarse—mark of the genetic defect Down's Syndrome. They were all retarded, some profoundly.

A few other students and teachers from Renascence filed in to take casual seats around one corner of the large, bright room. A final group came in, among them the director of Renascence who talked with a tall dark man who wore the colors of the Ministry on his chest.

When everyone was seated, the director stood, "We are honored this afternoon to have a very special guest—our Minister of Culture, Kurt Kraus.

Stoey's eyes were as big as her face, "Oh, David," she whispered, "I'm scared. What if he doesn't like my show?"

David stared at Kurt and did not answer.

By choice, Kurt sat between two of the retarded children. The little boy to his left seemed lost in a faraway place; the little girl to his right smiled up at him shyly. He smiled back, but his thoughts were bleak. He had called them the Forever Children once. He had looked at them and resented them, feeling that they usurped the place his brother should have had. Now, Eric had been gone for ninety years. And they would be gone too—because of him. He had taken the cards and dealt them out of the game.

The little girl touched his hand and smiled again. Sweet. Some of these children were so damned sweet, so full of love, you could almost feel it. In defense, he pulled his mind away and tried to fix it on the young dancer.

Stoey stood in front of the little audience, slim as a whisper in a brief practice dress that matched her large gray eyes. To Kurt, she looked as fragile as a young deer. Her voice was small and formal in the big room. "Hello. My name is Stoey. I'm going to show you how I work here at Renascence. I'm a choreographer."

The word met blank but pleasant looks from the children. Then somehow the barriers came down, and Stoey was a child talking to other children. "I make up dances in my head. Then, when I put them in here," she patted the console, "other people can learn the dance I made up.

"First, I think very hard about how I want things to look and then I program the machine. Sometimes I dance parts of it myself, to see how they feel. I'll show you."

She ran gracefully into the large space that separated her from her audience. "Let's say that I'm thinking about a cloud dance. I have to think about clouds, about how light they feel. And lightness is upward things. Everything has to lift. See?" An arm curved outward, palm up. She followed its line with a tilting head and upturned gaze. As they watched, she stretched slowly upward on one foot, extending the other so that her leg and body formed a beautiful rising line.

"When I have that all figured out, I put it into the machine." She ran lightly back to the console and quickly moved the controls. A stylized figure appeared and struck the pose she had demonstrated. "Then, I can look at it from all around and see how to make it better. And sometimes, when I try to do that, I make the dance too hard, so that people have to have joints and muscles in the wrong places. When I do that, the machine makes a terrible noise." She scrunched her little nose and put her hands on her hips, "It says, 'Bl-e-e-e-chh!' "

The children laughed.

"Now," she continued, "suppose somebody wants to learn the movement I just put in the machine. Well, they just put a sender around their neck and then set the machine on uni-vid in a practice room with mirrors. Then they step right inside." And to demonstrate, she pulled a small silver imager around her neck and running again to the center of the room, placed her body within the image as it held the pose. After an initial squawk from the machine, her body blended perfectly with the projection. She stood there for a moment, shimmering within the light image, until it seemed to Kurt that she was no more substantial, no more real, than moonbeams in water. Then, with a flip of her head, she moved out of the image and back to the console.

"And that's how I work until I have a whole dance inside. Now, I want to show you a dance I've just finished. David Defour wrote the music. It's just a tiny piece of his new conserere. My dance is about a girl who gets lost and wanders around on the banks of a creek, like the one here at Renascence. She's very lonesome because no one is there, and so she comes to a bank of clay and pours water on it until it's squishy, and then she makes herself a friend and then they dance together." She giggled. "David wanted me to call it 'Mud Pie,' but I didn't like that. I call it 'Clay Dancer.'" She turned to David anxiously and whispered, "Turn it on."

He did.

The soft, barely detectable throb of the motif began—the creek. Its waters pulsed against the moss-slick rocks and the sand that lined it and thrummed against the stony bed of the underlying mountain.

From the feel of it, Kurt knew at once that it was infrasound. Word of David's work had reached him, and when he experienced it at last, he knew it spoke of new directions for music, an interface with the Earth itself.

On the staging area, a figure lay prone and motionless. Another moved alone, running, searching, imploring with hesitant outstretched arms. Then the running figure knelt. Its hands began to play over the motionless form. Hands moved, kneaded, sculpted—a head, the lines of a back, an arm, another.

The figures reached for one another. Hands stretched out, touched, clasped. And then the two rose and began to dance. Colors defined them, changing them from dark solids to shimmering pastel ghosts who touched together, broke away, joined again.

Kurt smiled at the dance. It was simple; it was naive. And yet at the same time, it seemed somehow profound. It spoke of archetypes and mythos without knowing how or why it did so.

Beside him, the little retarded girl sat rigid. Her eyes held

fast to the kaleidoscopic figures as they whirled and leaped.
Kurt patted her hand and then abruptly felt the earth fall
away. Reality crumbled and another took its place.

*It was dusk. He stood in a heavily wooded ravine. At his
feet, a creek tumbled into the wild gorge below him. Dark was
falling fast. He had lost track of the time. He turned to go,
when something stopped him, something only dimly sensed,
something that caused the hair on the back of his neck to
crawl and prickle. A chill scurried over his spine and crept
into the marrow. Only his eyes moved, darting from side to
side, sweeping ground and tree limb, searching shadows. It
was behind him. Behind and above. He felt his heart pause,
then hammer at his throat. His senses strained.*

*Slowly, ever so slowly, he turned his head and stared into
the dark branches. Yellow eyes stared back. The mountain
lion's tawny body pressed in a crouch along the heavy oak
limb. He gasped.*

*Both sprang at once. He, to the opposite side of the creek,
splashing through icy water, sliding on moss-slick stones; the
cat, springing upward, gaining the treetops, plunging in the
opposite direction.*

*He ran. He ran, though he knew it was gone, knew he had
frightened it as it had frightened him. He ran and he could
not help himself, could not stop himself. He . . . .*

He looked around the room, dazed. The dance was finished. The child beside him sat limp. A dull cloud glazed her
eyes. Across the room, Stoey looked at him expectantly, as if
she tried to gauge his reaction.

He touched the seat that held him, moved a foot along
the floor, testing his reality, testing his sanity. And the floor
felt real, and the seat—but no more real, not *as* real, as the
gorge and the creek and the cat crouching in the shadows.

Shaken, he realized that people had spoken to him, had
spoken, and now waited for his reply. With an effort, he
pushed the experience toward the back of his mind and felt it
wait there, shrouding itself in mists and shadows.

They were standing and the director of Renascence was saying, "—and I know you'll want to meet David Defour."

And David was standing there, staring at him, saying stiffly, "I'm, uh, I was a friend of, uh, your wife."

"Of course," said Kurt, "we met before." He took David's hand. "I remember you." Then he said to the director, "If you'll excuse me for a while, I need to talk with this young man. He's one reason that I'm here." Kurt clasped his arm around David's shoulder and led him out on the wide deck overlooking the lake. He moved easily, while David held himself stiffly, as if he were ready to break and run at any moment.

They stopped near the railing. Below them, the surface of the water was broken by an advancing wedge of ducks in search of a handout. A mallard drake waggled his curly tail and quacked in anticipation. "I'm afraid we're going to disappoint them," said Kurt. The ducks broke formation and began to paddle in eccentric circles below them.

Without answering, David reached in his pocket and pulled out a small package of crackers. He crumbled one and tossed it in the water. The ducks plunged after the pieces. The losers squawked in rage.

"I'm very impressed with your music," said Kurt. "Very impressed."

A flush of pleasure crept over David's cheeks.

"You are the main reason I'm here."

The look of pleasure gave way to puzzlement. "Why?"

"Have you heard about the Ram?"

David nodded. "I guess everybody has."

"We're taking the world's great music aboard her. I especially want yours. I don't want the people to forget Earth, David. A thousand years from now, I want them to be able to listen to your music and remember."

David's mouth fell slightly open. A smile began to play at one corner of his lips, "Do you really think so? Do you really think they will?"

Kurt nodded. "It's important not to forget. It would be the tragedy of a caged animal, David. Without the remembering, it changes into something else. Something less. Do you understand?"

David looked across the lake to the mountains beyond. He stood leaning up against the railing for a time before he said, "I think so. I think we have to remember where we've been, and . . . And who was there with us."

A look came over David's face that was as faraway as space. Kurt wanted to reach out to him, break into that look somehow and probe it, but he held back, wondering if Liss walked in that memory. He was afraid she did. And he felt that anything he could say would be an unspeakable intrusion, a violation of a private thing, a stealthy look into someone else's soul. He walked away quietly and stood in the sun, feeling its warmth play over him, feeling the breeze against his face.

They stood there for a time and then David said, "I'd be honored to send my music on the Ram."

"Good." Kurt clasped his hand. "Your use of infrasound is amazing. The effects are—" He paused, feeling the memory stir again of a shadowy mountain lion in a river gorge. A cloud slid over the sun; a breeze shivered at the nape of his neck. He stood, still gripping David's hand, staring at a point beyond him. Finally his eyes met David's, "The effects are a little disconcerting. I felt the creek, the woods, through your music, and then, suddenly I was there. I felt—I saw a mountain lion."

David's eyes widened, narrowed, widened again. He started to speak, then turned away and stared at the lake before he said, "There *was* a mountain lion."

"Incredible," said Kurt. "I don't see how you got the effect."

"I was in the gorge. It was nearly dusk. I had forgotten the time." His hands touched the railing, slid back and forth along the rough wood, paused. "I turned to leave, and realized there was something there. Above me. Just behind me. All I could see were its eyes. I began to run—"

"And it ran in the other direction."

"I'd forgotten," said David. "I didn't remember it at all until just now. I was so scared, I didn't want to think about it. I forgot."

"But you taped it," said Kurt. "Somehow you captured it on tape."

"No," said David. "I made the tape this past winter. I saw the lion when I was twelve." His hands squeezed the railing, released, squeezed again. "I saw it more than six years ago."

Chapter 8

The linked solos sped far below the cave-riddled ridge called Lookout Mountain. Kurt swiveled to face Liss. "I don't want you going there."

She looked startled, "Why? It's my work—"

"We can find you work someplace else."

A quick flash of anger darkened her eyes, "I'm not a child. My work is important. It's important to me. It's not some toy you can take away and substitute with another." Her chin jutted in defiance.

"There's trouble on Vesta. It's not safe—"

"Of course there's trouble." Her voice was tinged with exasperation. "That's why I'm going. You can't expect an investigative reporter to sit in Chatlanta and get a decent insight into Vestan politics, can you?"

He looked at her keenly as the small linked cars plunged through the lighted tunnel. "You're fond of old quotations, Liss. Try this one: 'Discretion is the better part of valor.' "

"I don't see it as valor at all. I see it as my job."

"Liss, there are people in the belt who might try to get at me through you. They'd like nothing better than to place you in a compromising situation in order to embarrass the Ministry."

Her lips pressed together for a moment before she said, "You don't give me much credit for common sense, Kurt," adding stiffly, "It isn't my plan to embarrass you."

"And I don't think you're giving the enemies of the Ministry much credit. This isn't a game, Liss."

"You act as if it is. You give me vague warnings about dire but nebulous consequences and not one hard fact to go along with it. Well, I'm sick of being treated like a child. If the facts are to be had, I'll find them myself."

The solos pulled up to a side slot and stopped. They got out in silence and took the sublif to the surface, emerging to bright sunlight and the low grass and spreading old trees of the Moccasin Bend Pleasance. The Crystal Center, mushrooming beyond them, caught the rays of the sun; people moved through its interior like tiny fish in a curving aquarium. Liss stared at it, "I never get tired of seeing old buildings like this. It gives me a sense of history—of the continuity of things."

Kurt wondered again at the gulf between them. When he was her age, he had never dreamed of such a building. Not for ninety years would one be built. And now it had stood for over a century. Yet, it did give a feeling of continuity. It was a landmark in a sequence of years that tended to blur into indistinctness as if he looked at them through a dim, streaked glass. And there were others: a stark camp where children lived behind barbed wire; a ceremony where he received the ribbons of his office; Renascence and a warm fire after a bone-chilling day in the snow—and the Ram.

He wondered at it. The landmarks of his life were man-made. The oceans rolled on against beaches that grew and receded; mountains slowly rose, slowly crumbled; the very earth shifted beneath his feet, yet though his body had within it the potential to live on beyond these things of nature, his mind had never fully grasped it. He would live for a hundred years more, and after that, he would live another hundred. And how many years would he be within the curving walls of the Ram? He looked at Liss as they walked across the wide lawn toward the outdoor concert hall. He hadn't told her yet about the Ram, hadn't told her yet that he was leaving.

The sun played against the feathery waves of her hair and shone like pale fire. Come with me, little girl, he wanted to say. Come with me. But he didn't. It wouldn't be fair. She might do it out of a misplaced sense of obligation, or even fondness, but it wasn't enough. Not enough.

They came to the pavillion where their table waited. They took their places and in a few minutes their selections began to arrive. They lunched on a Szechuan dish hot with pepper and onions, cooling it with a white wine that drew its taste from flinty soil. And then Liss said, "It's going to be strange, seeing David again after all this time. I think I'm nervous." She stared at her plate for a moment, "Nervous for me, nervous for him too. It's awfully important to David, isn't it? Couldn't this concert be a turning point?"

Kurt nodded. "But don't be too nervous for him. His music has already been heard by a lot of important people. "Earth Song" is something new in music, Liss. Something different. I'm taking it with me on the Ram—" And it was out. That quickly he had told her without intending to. He, who always weighed each word, had hurled these at her as if they were stones.

She sat very still. She held her face tilted away as if she had been struck.

He stared at her, not knowing what to say, saying nothing.

"So you're going with the Ram," she finally said. "It's leaving very soon."

He nodded.

"Had you intended to tell me at all? Or was I just going to receive a transmission someday: 'Having a wonderful time. See you in a dozen millennia or so.' "

"I've hurt you. I didn't mean to."

Her lips pressed together. She raised her chin and leveled her eyes at him. "Oh, don't worry about that. You've already done well on that account today."

He looked at her; he didn't speak.

"It works at your convenience, doesn't it, Kurt? This marriage contract. Let's invoke it by all means if my presence on Vesta might embarrass you. On the other hand, don't bother to mention to your wife that you're planning a little trip for the next half-eternity."

"I'm sorry, Liss. I was going to tell you."

She took a swallow of wine, set the glass down briskly and
drew out a small recorder. "I can't pass up this opportunity,
can I? A chance to interview the Prime Minister of the Ram."
Her eyes flashed with hurt, with anger. "You will be the Prime
Minister, won't you?"

He reached out and took her hand. She snatched it away
and stabbed a code into the little recorder. "Tell me, Citizen
Kraus, why did you decide to go with the Ram? Adventure?
Boredom perhaps?"

He stared at her. Why was he going? Was it because he
hoped to revive that small hard core of himself that had died
so long ago? But maybe it wasn't dead. Not altogether. Maybe
the Ram was a force that could regenerate. And then he could
create again, he thought. He could create a new milieu. A
new home for humankind—one without boundaries.

When he was fifteen years old, he had had to turn his
back on the world and look toward a new one. It was a matter
of survival. It still was; people had to move on.

"Tell me, Citizen Kraus," said Liss. "Why you?"

He looked at her, then down at his hands with the fingers
splayed against the tabletop. He sat looking at them for a few
moments before he said, "I had no choice." He had never had
a choice, it seemed. When he was fifteen years old he had
inherited a mantle of leadership. Fifteen, and he had carried
it ever since. It was too late for him now, too late to lay it
down.

Her voice cut. "Was it ego, Kurt?"

Survival. He wanted to say "survival," but he didn't. Was
there a difference? Could a man survive if his ego crumbled
to nothing? Uneasy memories circled at the back of his mind.
But there had to be a purpose. There had to be a reason why
he had lived. There had to be a justification. Yet, even as the
thought came, another followed: Really? Or was his "purpose"
nothing more than the vain cry of a damaged ego?—a pitiful
attempt to rationalize an irrelevant existence?

Crap. Was it irrelevance that created Renascence? Irrelevance that made the Ramirez Star Drive possible? He smiled
grimly, inwardly, at his pitying self-indulgence. He had inherited the Earth—and in pretty bad shape, at that. It wasn't

perfect—hell no—but it was a geometric improvement over what it had been. He looked at Liss. "Maybe it was ego that made me decide. Maybe not. But we do what we have to do, don't we?"

Her eyes were cool blue mirrors; he couldn't read what lay behind them. "Are you sure, Kurt?"

Sure? Could he be sure? Had he ever really been sure about anything? Or had it all been a crap-shoot, with the only sure thing his own illusions about himself? And did it matter? He finally nodded. "I'm going with the Ram, Liss."

They finished their meal in polite silence. Each one of them sat behind a private wall. They nodded and smiled at passers-by and watched across the sunlit lawn as musicians and technicians began to assemble for the concert.

Then Liss saw a small group of people moving slowly across the grass. Squinting against the glare, she stared, then jumped up. "It's David!" She began to run across the wide lawn toward him.

Liss slowed her tumultuous dash; then she stopped. David watched her from across the lawn. They looked at one another for a few moments and then began to move again. They met in the middle of the field, and when they came close, both stopped. "Hello," said Liss.

"Hello."

"It's a big day for you," and she thought, how stupid that sounded, how silly. It was something to say to a child.

But he nodded gravely and said, "Yes." And then he said, "Let's walk. I mean, I can't stand still. We've got a while. Let's walk."

They moved together through the springy grass. He seemed to her to be made of coiled wires bursting into energy. "Slow down," she said. "Where are we going?"

He stopped and stared around him. "Anywhere. I can't stand still. Nervous."

He looked pale to her. "Are you all right?"

A hand flew to his mouth. He moaned. "I'm going to be sick." He began to lope toward the public toilets across the lawn. She stood uncertainly for a moment and then began to run along behind, stopping again as he dashed inside and disappeared behind the rapidly closing door.

He emerged a few minutes later, paler than ever, and sweaty. Much of the tension in his body seemed to have eased. He flopped to the grass and lay back, shutting his eyes against the sun.

She sat down beside him. "Are you better now?"

He nodded, "I think so," but didn't look at her. They sat silently until out of nothing he said, "I didn't mean to puke. I thought about seeing you again, for a long time. I thought about all the things I was going to say. And then—when the time comes—I puke."

Her lips quirked in a smile. "So, I make you sick?"

He looked at her in horror. "Oh, no! Not you. It's the concert." He sat up, cross-legged, in the grass. His hands began to pull against one another, bulging the smooth muscles of his forearms, his biceps. He seemed to concentrate on the pull and release of tension. With each tug, he breathed in; when he relaxed the pull, his breath shuddered raggedly out.

Liss watched in fascination. "Does that relax you?"

"I'm not sure. It keeps me from thinking about puking."

"Oh, David. Are you always like this before a concert?"

"I don't know. This is my first. My first real one, anyway." He stared at her. "What if it isn't any good? What if nobody likes it?"

"They *will* like it. Kurt said so."

"Did he really?"

She nodded. Poor David. He couldn't be more nervous if he walked on a tightrope over a pit filled with poisonous snakes and daggers, she thought. "What did you intend to say to me when you saw me, David?"

"I don't know. Different things. You know."

"Like what?"

"Like. . . . You know. How are you? Things like that." He resumed the tug of war between his hands.

"I'm fine, David," she said softly.

"I saw your baby," he blurted.

"Oh." A startled look passed over her face, followed by a quick flash of pain. She looked away. "I don't see her often," she said. "It's not allowed, you know." And in that moment, she wanted to tell him, wanted to say, "She's yours too." But she couldn't. What was the point? It would only make him feel a guilt that he didn't deserve. She wasn't going to do that to him; she wasn't going to give him the chance to know why she had married Kurt.

"She . . . she looks like you," he said.

"I suppose she does." And if Alani had been the image of David, would he have seen it? She looked at him as he sprawled on the grass. How young he seemed. He was still a boy. "Kurt's going away on the Ram," she said without knowing why.

He seemed startled. "Then you'll be going too."

She shook her head. "No."

"But, why? He'll—Kurt—will want you to." He pronounced Kurt's name carefully, as if the word bristled with barbs.

The words began to spill out of her mouth then, as if in the saying she could convince herself of the truth. "I'm just in his way. A little girl. Not anything more, really. I'm just a little girl to him." Tears began to mist her eyes. She blinked them away. "That's all I am."

He looked at her uneasily, as if he didn't know what to say.

She wished she hadn't spoken. She felt ashamed, as if she had betrayed someone. And yet, she wasn't sure who it was she betrayed. She didn't want to meet David's eyes. Instead she looked around her at the people passing by, at the fluffy clouds that floated in the hot blue sky. Nearby, she saw a girl standing, watching them—a young girl, no more than twelve or so, with serious gray eyes and an elfin heart-shaped face. "Who's that?" she asked.

David looked up, then said, "Oh, that's Stoey. From Renascence."

There was something about the girl, something in the way she watched the two of them. She doesn't think much of me at all, thought Liss. She wishes that I'd go away. David lay in the grass, oblivious to the little girl. "She likes you," said Liss.

"What?"

"Stoey. She's in love with you."

Bewilderment crossed his face. "She's just a kid. She's nothing but a child."

She stared at him. Damn you, David, she thought. Damn you for saying that. With a quick stab of pity for the little girl who watched them, Liss stood up and brushed off her clothes. She looked down at David then. "Don't ever tell her that," she said. Then she turned and walked quickly away.

From his table in the pavilion, Kurt watched Liss and David in the distance. When she walked away from David, Kurt thought that she would come back and sit with him until the concert began. Instead, she headed in the opposite direction, toward the river. Finally, she was no more than a tiny figure standing alone beneath a spreading oak that hung its branches low over the water.

A man stepped up to him, "Citizen Kraus," he said formally, "your box is ready."

He rose and followed the man toward the concert arena, but when they approached the lifter that led to the reserved boxes high above the other seats, Kurt paused. Across the way, he saw the Director of Renascence and two other adults lead a small group of children to their seats. The children were retarded, several with the stigmata of Down's Syndrome. They were new, he thought. They were on their way to Renascence for the first time. "I've changed my mind," he said to the man beside him. "Give my box to someone else." He turned away from the startled man and walked across to the little group.

He greeted the Director and then took a seat between two of the children. He felt especially attracted to the little black boy at his left. He wasn't more than seven or eight, with shy dark eyes that were slanted at the corners, the lids creased with an epicanthal fold.

Kurt read the boy's name tag. "Michael," he said, "we're going to hear some wonderful music."

The boy smiled up at him, but he didn't speak. Kurt wondered if he could. He smiled back and ruffled the boy's soft curly hair with his big hand. "Do you like music, Michael?"

The boy looked at him in silence, then began to suck his

thumb. Kurt took the child's other hand in his, spreading it open gently. The palm was pale pink; a single crease—the simian crease—ran diagonally across its surface. The boy's fingers curled trustingly around his.

The orchestra and the visiographers filed into the arena. Across the way, David Defour perched tensely in the box next to Kurt's empty chair. Although he scanned the others in the box with David, Kurt saw no sign of Liss, nor did he see her on the banks of the river, though he looked until the music began.

Rousseau, the famous conductor—the Renascence conductor, Kurt amended mentally—entered. After the first excited rustle of applause, an expectant hush fell over the audience.

Within the arena, the magic of the visiographers blotted out the sun. It grew as black as night, as black as space, as the nearly invisible mesh above polarized. The silence was electric. Kurt's skin seemed to tingle, and the air felt different in his nostrils. A change in ionization, he thought, a magic change. The boy felt it, too. He clasped his hands together in excitement.

Into the charged blackness exploded a silent fireball, swirling and compressing as he watched into a gaseous swollen disc. A sound began to throb, a sound so faint, so subtle, as to be more felt than heard.

Genesis, he thought. It was the beginning of the Earth.

The glowing disc grew dimmer, more opaque now. Soon it was a sphere whirling in a giddy wheeling race around the sun.

The sound intensified. Thick clouds swirled over the surface of the globe. Then as he watched, they thinned and broke here and there—and the full Earth bloomed.

The scene shifted to a single sea rolling out before him, shimmering away toward a blood-red horizon. The throbbing changed subtly. It whispered against his ears, insinuated itself in his brain. It was the sound of wind and tide—and something more—the sound of the underlying earth echoing through the water.

And then a delicate instrumental sound—a hint of melody, an answering harmonic, and then a swelling of sound and a lifting of the rocky core of the planet.

The volcano boiled at the surface of the sea and rose in bubbling life before him, steaming under the breakers as the sound grew into music.

The scene shifted again and small plants crept on the surface of bare rock. And creatures came. A million creatures passed—a million years.

Mountains wore away before his eyes and then he saw, he felt the blue ridge of Renascence. It sang to him of mists and memories.

Michael stirred beside him. In the dimness, Kurt could see the boy's arms extended rigidly along his body. The child's eyes were open and staring.

Frightened, thought Kurt. Poor little kid. He reached out and took the child's hand in his.

The earth crumbled beneath him and fell away. The boundaries of his reality, he saw were only tissue. And as he watched, they shredded and dissolved.

He walked alone in Renascence. It was twilight. Although the setting sun sent gold and rose to play against the mountains, a heavy gray mist seemed to shroud the light.

She was leaving. Liss was leaving him.

The dying sun sent a bright shaft through the mist. It blazed against the broken symbol of infinity on the ring he wore; it played against the ring and taunted him. He grasped it, tried to pull it off, but it was too tight.

He walked through the woods without knowing where he was going, without caring. He found himself crossing a small creek, stepping from stone to stone, feeling the cold water seep inside his shoes to chill him.

He looked up. Tanya Rolfe's cabin lay just ahead. Tanya. He wanted to see Tanya.

He pushed her cabin door open, stepped inside.

She sat beside the open window. A gentle breeze lifted a lock of her hair. It rose and fell in the blaze of the dying sun. Rose and fell. Rose and fell.

Nothing else moved.
Nothing. ; .
He lay for hours in the blackness, pressing his body
against the earth. He lay near the torn body of the little fawn.
The smell of the earth was in his nostrils; the taste of his salt
tears lay against his tongue.
And in the distance, a hungry bobcat waited. . .

He struggled to his feet. The rapt audience still sat under the spell of "Earth Song." Dazed, he stared around him feeling dizzy and displaced as if he had fallen into an alien land.

He turned and stumbled out of the arena, only half-aware of what he did. The smell of damp earth still clung to his nostrils—the smell of damp earth, and the warm blood of a little deer.

He ran into the blaze of an afternoon sun that could not dry the tears that were streaming down his face.

David's face was white and strained as he tried to absorb what Kurt had told him. "It wasn't on the infrasound tapes. Do you think I'm so cold-blooded that I go around taping the death of my friends?"

"I don't know what I think about it," said Kurt, "but something is on those tapes. Something that put me on a direct line to your experience."

Liss sat quietly in the corner of the little private room in the Crystal Center. She had gone to the reception after the concert only to find that the guest of honor and the chief dignitary were missing. A puzzled aide had led her to them. Liss looked at Kurt speculatively. "Why don't you play the tapes again and see what happens this time?"

They looked at her. "We could have audio set up easily," said David, "but the visiog would be a problem."

"Let's try it," said Kurt.

They sent out for a light supper and ate while technicians made the adjustments under the orders of the aide who fluttered in and out of the room with a distracted look on her face. Once, she approached them and said, "The guests are getting very restless."

After a brief foray into the reception, which overjoyed the aide, they gathered back in the little room. David worked the controls that had been hastily attached to the Communicator console and began the tapes at the point where Kurt had become aware of the mountains of Renascence.

They listened in silence. This time, Kurt felt the mountains again, but that was all—only the haunting strains of David's music played against his senses. "Nothing," he said at last.

"Maybe it was just an illusion," said Liss, "something brought on at the moment."

"No." David looked at Kurt. "He described everything in Tanya's room. Everything. Exactly as it was the night she died."

Liss's brow furrowed. "It doesn't make any sense."

"Maybe it's the visiog," said David, "maybe it needs both."

Kurt leaned back and stared thoughtfully at the wall. "I don't think so," he said finally. "The first time was at Renascence. There wasn't any visiog then—only the little girl's dance figures. But something triggered it. What?" he said softly. "What?"

"Maybe if you try to recreate everything that happened. . . . Maybe you'll remember something," said Liss.

Kurt closed his eyes and tried to recall the first time. "I came into the Common Hall with the director and sat down. I was directly opposite the projection—no—a little to the left. I sat on the front row because of the children—" He stopped. "The children—There was a child, a little girl, just to my right. I took her hand." He stood up and began to pace around the room. "The children—" he said again.

"I don't understand," said Liss.

"The Forever Children," said Kurt, "the little retarded children. I sat with them again today. There was a little boy, Michael, with Down's Syndrome. I talked to him and looked at his palm. And then during the concert I touched him again. That's when it happened."

The blank look on Liss's face gave way to incredulity. "Are you saying that those children caused this to happen?"

"I'm not saying anything, yet," said Kurt, "but I'm going to find out."

The aide who delivered the child stood uncertainly at the door. Kurt took the little boy's hand and led him into the room. "You can go now," he said to the aide. "We'll call if we need you."

The child deposited a thumb in his mouth and looked up at Kurt trustingly.

"I've got something for you," said Kurt, smiling at the boy. "Cakes and cookies and some punch. Let's sit over here." He offered Michael a chunk of cake.

The boy stared at it for a moment. Then the thumb came out of his mouth, and he reached for it. When he had reduced it to crumbs and a pink streak of icing on his chin, Liss gave him a little glass of punch, guiding his hand with hers. "He's cute, Kurt. Really sweet."

"Now, we're going to listen to some music, Michael. Would you like that?" asked Kurt. He felt a little ashamed of himself for exploiting the boy, but he had to know. "Begin the tape that I heard at Renascence," he told David.

After a few adjustments, David switched it on.

Kurt looked at the little black boy beside him—the flicker of shame again. But, he had to know. He took the child's hand in his. . . .

And reality shattered.

. . . *It was behind him. Behind and above. He felt his heart pause, then hammer at his throat. His senses strained.*

Slowly, ever so slowly, he turned his head and stared into the dark branches.

Yellow eyes stared back. . . .

The room lay in silence. Kurt blinked and stared around him. David's hand still lay on the controls.

Liss gave a ragged sigh. Her eyes were round and very blue; her voice was no more than a whisper, "I was there, Kurt. I saw it. The mountain lion—"

He stared at her. She sat across the room; she hadn't touched the boy.

A curious look crossed David's face. "I felt something, too. Something. It wasn't like being there. It was more like remembering. And I didn't want to. That's why I shut it off."

Liss's voice was very small. "What is it, Kurt?"

He looked at the child beside him. Michael lay back, staring at nothing. His thumb was in his mouth. "I don't know." Somehow the experience—the buried memory of the mountain lion—had funneled through this child into their minds. And somehow it had been triggered by the infrasound itself. Yet, that didn't make sense. How could the infrasound cause it? Unless—the thought was staggering—unless it was there all along.

He rubbed tense fingers over a furrowed brow. It was unbelievable. But that was the only thing that made any sense. "I think this child—these children—are empaths."

"Empaths!" Liss's voice was startled. "You mean they can read minds?"

"I don't know. Maybe not. Maybe it's only emotions—and pictures. But I think it's there all the time. I think they receive and send continuously on a very low level."

"You mean, right now?" David stared at the little boy.

Kurt nodded. "But we never knew it before. Your infrasound augmented it somehow. Amplified it."

"If it's emotions that they send," said Liss, "then maybe it's still low-level even with the infrasound enhancing it. What we picked up wasn't an everyday sort of feeling."

"No," said David. "I recall it being rather heavy-duty, as far as feelings go."

"That's what I mean," Liss went on. "Maybe it has to be a really powerful emotion for us to pick it up. Maybe only the strongest emotions come through."

"But I'd forgotten it," said David. "It was gone. How did he pick it up?"

"You didn't forget," said Kurt quickly. "You repressed it

because you didn't want to remember. But it was there. It was always there."

"Repressed memories are always traumatic," added Liss. "Painful. Scary. That's why they're repressed to begin with."

David shook his head, "I still don't understand it."

Kurt stared at him sharply, "You were there. You were recording in the same place that you'd seen the lion years before. Unconsciously, you were reliving it. The same thing must have happened with Tanya's death.

David raised an eyebrow, "That part of 'Earth Song' was a recording of Wolf Creek, not Tanya's cabin. I was walking along the stones on the creek bottom. I remember, because I slipped. I had to grab the bridge to keep from falling—"

"And the bridge is just under Tanya's window," said Liss quickly. "You found Tanya by that window. The tape recorded what must have been in your mind."

He looked from Liss to Kurt, "You mean a sort of harmonic?"

"Enough for Michael to pick up."

David frowned in concentration. "I still don't see how it works. If the tape picked up the experience, where does Michael come in? If he is an empath, why would he pick up just what was on the tape? Why wouldn't he get other feelings? Unless—" Suddenly he stared at the little boy and began to grin widely. "He isn't the empath. The infrasound is. Michael is the focus—the amplifier." He reached for the boy's hand. "When you touched him, maybe the sweat on your hand altered the resistance and helped you pick it up."

"But I was across the room," said Liss. "I felt it too."

"So did I," admitted David. "But I don't think either of us picked up as much as Kurt did." He looked around the room. "There aren't any distractions here. Maybe that's why we felt it. In a crowd—or an audience—we might not have noticed it."

"It's frightening," said Liss in a low voice. "Parts of your memory caught on tape. Things you didn't really want to remember, but that are stronger than anything else inside you."

Her eyes looked very grave to Kurt. He remembered a

look he'd seen in them before—eyes that stared wildly at nothing. *Awful, awful, awful. Oh, God! Awful.* "I wonder," he said slowly, "if your recorder works on people."

"What do you mean?" asked David.

"I mean, I wonder if an individual's infrasound could be picked up and broadcast. Could it?"

David thought for a moment, then he said, "I could try. I'd have to narrow the band a lot. It would be a very subtle sound."

"Do it," said Kurt. "Will you be our volunteer?" he asked Liss lightly.

She raised an eyebrow. "It won't make me radioactive or anything, will it?"

David laughed. "It's harmless."

"Well, I'm not really enthusiastic about it," she said. Then she grinned. "But, in the interest of science, you can go ahead."

He calibrated dials, one against the other, while the child, Michael, lay back, sucking his thumb, staring at nothing. "I think I'm ready. Just sit there, Liss. It won't hurt, I promise."

At first the dials pulsed soundlessly. Then, with a touch, David moved the transmission into the audible range.

Sinew glided against sinew. Blood ebbed and flowed through arteries that throbbed with the movement of tiny muscle fibers in their walls. Nerves sang as cells whispered chemicals from tiny pulsing walls.

And with a gasp, the three plunged into the rotting depths of Vesta's Labyrinth.

White-faced and shaken, Liss excused herself, "I'm going to bed, Kurt. I don't want to think about this anymore."

He looked up in concern. It had taken nearly an hour to calm her. The memories of the Labyrinth had flooded them, nearly drowned them. Only little Michael seemed untouched. He had plopped in a tumbled heap with his thumb in his mouth, his forefinger gently caressing his nose. Now, he slept. The thumb had slipped away from his half-open mouth. He breathed evenly. "I'll go with you, Liss," said Kurt.

"No," she said. "You're not ready to go yet, and I want to

be alone for a while. It's only a few minutes by solo. I'll be all right."

"If you're sure. . . ." he said.

She nodded and left the room.

When she had gone, Kurt looked at David. "Now that you know what happened in the Labyrinth, I'm going to tell you the rest. I'm going to need your help. And his—" He looked at the sleeping boy.

They talked the rest of the night. They talked until dawn crept into the room, and then they ordered breakfast. After they ate, they gave Michael over to the aide for a bath and a change of clothes.

"I could use a bath too," said Kurt, "and a few hours sleep. We'll need it before we leave for Vesta."

"Do you really think we'll get the proof we need about Silvio?" asked David.

"Maybe we won't need to," said Kurt. He went over to the Communicator console and punched a code. The female voice answered, "Waiting."

"Priority 0721. Reservations. Next skiptor to Vesta."

"Confirmed. Next scheduled departure, this date, eighteen-hundred hours."

Kurt stared at the console. He ought to tell Liss. She'd want him to. He punched the code again.

She didn't answer. Then the override came on. In dismay, he read the note she had left him:

Kurt dear,
        When you read this, I will be on my way to Vesta. I felt it was important before, but now that I know, now that I remember, I have to go. I have no choice.
        I'll get the proof. I know it.
        Remember what you said to me: we do what we have to do.

Liss

Ice formed in the pit of his stomach. With hands that

shook, he coded the communicator and sent a priority communique to the Ram.

MY WIFE IS TRAVELING ALONE. PLEASE
OFFER HER EVERY COURTESY. . . . KRAUS.

He hoped Jacoby would understand his message; he prayed Jacoby would get it in time.

Chapter 9

The late afternoon Dayglow sent slanting light into the play arena. Liss stood watching a group of children wearing the buff uniform of the twelve-to fourteen-year-olds of Vesta Central. They were playing Snakes and Sails.

The play arena had been transformed into a miniature alien landscape. Craggy scarps and fissures of gray rock stretched into the horizon. A steaming acid-green sea lapped against a rocky shore. On a broken plateau in the center of the area stood Earth Base I. Suddenly, red lights flashed. Sirens squawked. Earth Base was under attack.

Deadly alien Snakes, each under the control of a child from Team B, began to slither in preplanned formation from hidden fissures. Tiny human figures emerged from Earth Base I, soaring on silver-winged, programmed gliders that bore exotic weapons.

A thick-bodied viper emerged from a crevasse near Earth Base. Its ugly triangular head moved in response to the heat of the man who glided on silver wings overhead. The Snake's eyes glittered. Its mouth fell open and a forked tongue slithered out. The glider banked, but it was too late. Deadly disinto rays sprayed from each prong of the forked tongue. The glider dissolved and the tiny man fell screaming into the acid sea.

Another glider swooped in at a steep angle and took aim with a vibro gun. Blue tracers showed that the aim was true— the delicate brain cage at the back of the serpent's throat. The Snake's disintos turned traitor. The forked tongue curled in upon itself and fired. The creature destructed in a blaze of red.

Liss stared at the children. They were about the age of the ones she had seen in the Labyrinth—in that awful place. She was sure that all the children on Vesta were taken there for those hideous ceremonies.

Another Snake destructed. Another. Yells of triumph erupted from Team A. The enemy was routed. She looked at them in wonder. They seemed so normal. It was hard to believe that these very children could have been part of that chanting, mindless group. She remembered the boy they raised on the giant silver T—the boy whose neck had been snapped as she watched. How many had died? How many more? Uneasily, she watched the children begin to file away from the play arena. One of these? Which one would be next?

If only she could get one to talk. One witness. That's all she needed. She had had no definite plan, but now one began to hatch as she watched the children. She stepped up to a boy who stood alone. "Hello," she said, "I'd like to talk with you."

"What about?" He had straight blond hair that fell in his eyes. He brushed his hair aside with a thin hand and stared at her curiously with pale eyes that were somewhere between gray and blue.

"I'm a reporter," she said. "I'm going to pick a student, and then write about him—what he does all day, what he's interested in."

"Me?" He seemed pleased at the attention.

"Maybe you. If what you tell me is interesting enough."

"Oh, I know all kinds of interesting stuff."

"How about places," asked Liss casually. "Know any special places on Vesta? You know, where people don't usually go?"

"Sure. Lots. Is your story going to be on three-vee?"

Liss nodded. "Three-vee. Maybe even an arena show."

A skeptical look came over his face. "I don't see any equipment."

Sharp kid. "I have to do my preliminaries first. I need to talk with you. Get to know you. Later on, we bring in the equipment."

He narrowed his eyes. "I don't know. You don't have any equipment. I got things to do." He turned away.

"Wait."

He looked back over his shoulder.

"Don't go. If you go, you won't be on three-vee. You'd be special. I'll bet nobody else in your dorm has been on three-vee."

He stopped, turned around slowly, and stared at her. A crafty look crossed his face. "What'll you give me if I talk to you?"

Rotten kid. Of all the kids on Vesta she had to pick this one. "What do you want?"

He looked her up and down. "Something. Something you got."

She stared at him in disbelief. He was actually trying to proposition her. Then, she nearly laughed. The boy's face had worked itself into a leer that was a creditable replica of Mark Mirage—and that line, she recalled, was out of one of his old three-vee shows.

With an effort, she kept her face solemn. She had him now; she remembered the rest of the scenario: the beautiful temptress and Mark Mirage were in cahoots, undercover agents in league against the vicious Kahrattans, the galactic criminal gang. "We have to be careful," she said in a low voice, "the skies have eyes."

His eyes widened, then he nodded gravely.

"My name is Liss." She paused expectantly.

"I'm Steven."

"Of course you are, Steven. We've had our eye on you."

"You have?"

She nodded. "We needed someone smart and brave. I knew you were our man when I first saw you. When I saw how you dived your glider and zapped the alien Snake, I knew you would be cool in a crisis."

"You did?" He looked from side to side cautiously, then he said in a low voice, "What's going on?"

"Sh-h-h. The spheres have ears."

He nodded and fell in beside her. As they walked along together, he looked at her expectantly. "Where're we going?"

"To the Labyrinth."

"Oh," said Steven with something close to awe.

They walked together through the streets of Vesta. Once, Liss stopped and bought a tempo-light. She was going to need it in the cave-room, she thought. She stuffed the little foil-wrapped package in her pocket, and they went on.

She felt uneasy as they entered the Labyrinth. The type of people she saw there made her feel slightly unclean by proximity.

The scent of warm sweat and musk permeated every breath she drew. Underneath lay secondary scents of oils and powders that could offer oblivion for a few minutes—or forever.

She found her breath coming quicker and quicker as she penetrated the twisting corridors. A blazing pink rose flashed from a wall at eye level ahead of her. She recoiled, staring as it reformed into an obscenity. Steven's eyes were huge, "We're not allowed in here," he said. "We have to sneak."

They came to an intersection where the corridors splayed out in five directions. Which way? She was trying to get back to the tunnel and the chute that had dropped her into the cave-room, but now she was confused. All of the passageways looked alike.

A robovendor brushed against her, its multi-hands reached out in an obscene embrace. "Massage?" it purred. She pushed it away and stared at the intersection. Which way?

She pulled Steven into an alcove, "There's a place we need to go. You've been there. It's a big room. Very big. Where the children have, uh, meetings. Do you know where I mean?"

"You mean, the Pioneer meetings?"

She looked at him. "I'm not sure what you call them. It's a large room. Cut out of rock. There's a big bowl—a sort of saucer in the center."

"Oh, sure. That's where we go for Pioneers." He looked at her curiously. "We never go this way."

"Oh. Well, there's a secret entrance from up here," she said, "but this time, maybe we'd better go your way."

He nodded. "Then we'd better go down a level," he said, and added with bravado, "I'll get us there."

The room was vast, larger than she had remembered. It seems bigger because it's empty, she thought. At least she didn't have to use the tempo-light. The room was dim, but she could see well enough. Light reflected from the shallow metal bowl that stood near them in the center of the room.

She found herself starting at shadows. Her voice bounced off the gray rock walls and echoed in her ears when she said, "Steven, I really need your help now. I want you to trust me. I want you to tell me what goes on in this room. Everything."

He looked puzzled.

"Tell me, Steven."

"Well, it's just meetings. Nothing much. Just meetings."

She looked at him closely. His eyes were fixed on hers. The puzzled look remained. She felt her heart sink. He really couldn't tell her; he really didn't remember.

But, was that so surprising? She hadn't remembered either—not until the infrasound jarred it all loose. "Oh, damn," she said under her breath. She had been so sure that he could tell her.

But then, maybe he could. She looked at him speculatively. Maybe. "Steven, what I'm going to tell you may sound weird, but I want you to trust me."

He nodded uncertainly.

She swallowed and prayed he'd believe her. "You're carrying valuable intelligence locked in your mind, Steven. And I, as your operative, have come to retrieve it."

His eyes tracked hers; they were very round.

"You don't remember this, but we gave you a drug to forget. It was for your protection. For all of our protection," she added quickly. "Now I'm going to put you to sleep, Steven, and then you'll remember. All right?"

His eyes were huge. He nodded.

She didn't know much at all about hypnosis. She tried to remember what little she *did* know. Eye strain. That was part of it. She needed something glittery.

She remembered the tempo-light and pulled it out of her

pocket. She tore away the foil and thumbed the light on. "I'm going to shine this light in your eyes, Steven."

His pupils contracted sharply in the glare of the light. He squeezed his eyes shut.

"You've got to help me, Steven."

"I'm sorry."

Her light glittered on the silver foil wrapping that had dropped to the floor. Suddenly she had an idea. "Look, Steven, I'll shine the light on the foil. You can look at that instead and it won't be so bright." As she picked it up, something suggested itself to her. Her fingers moved over the foil, folding and crimping it into a shape. "There," she said. She began to play her light over the glittering crumpled surface. "Look at the silver T, Steven. Look at the silver T."

She watched his eyes as he stared at the little foil T. His pupils contracted at the brightness, then dilated. "Look at it, Steven. Watch it closely. Watch and remember, watch and remember. . . ."

The boy stared at the foil. His eyes began to glaze.

"Watch and remember," said Liss. "Watch and remember."

The whispering began as if it came from deep within her brain. ". . . Silver T . . . Silver T. . . ."

She stared around her.

". . . Silver T . . . Silver T. . . ."

A brilliant white shaft of light blazed upward from the metal bowl, blinding her. The whisper rose in volume, ". . . Silver T . . . Silver T. . . ."

The white light became a flaming silver cross.

She stood frozen as a voice said, "Steven. You are to leave now. You are to go directly to your room. Then you will sleep."

The boy's eyes were glazed and fixed on the huge silver T. Without a word, he turned and walked toward the door.

"Wait," cried Liss.

He walked on as if he hadn't heard her. Then he was gone.

"Clever, Citizeness," said the voice, "but not enough."

She whirled at the sound and stared into the eyes of Silvio

Tarantino. They were round and very black. They gave back
no light as they stared into hers. A smile—gentle, almost
cherublike—played across his lips.

Then she realized that she looked at a projection.

His hand went to the heavy silver T at his throat. He
touched first one link of the chain, then another. Although
she heard nothing, she thought she saw his lips move slightly,
thought she saw a subtle swelling in his throat. She stared for
a moment more. He could see her, she knew, but if he were
some distance from her, maybe she could get away.

She began to run, plunging wildly toward the door. It
pushed open against her weight, and she half-fell into the
corridor outside.

There were two men waiting for her there. Two men who
wore heavy silver T's around their necks.

Horror danced in her eyes. Then came the insane
thought: "The skies have eyes." She heard herself begin to
laugh. And she couldn't stop until her laughter turned into
gasping sobs.

They took her into the Labyrinth to a place with a silken
door. The rough stone walls were pocked and cratered from
the play of shadows and flickering lights. A faint smell of flowers and rot permeated the air.

The two men led her into a dim room to the man waiting
there. His eyes lay in a stripe of shadow. His lips moved. "Ah,
Citizeness. How nice of you to come."

She stared in fascination at the lips that moved in the dim
light, at the elliptical birth mark that pulsed at the angle of his
jaw, at the silver T that lay at the hollow of his throat.

"It's unfortunate that you remembered, unfortunate that
you tried to subvert the boy."

Subvert. She trembled on the edge of hysteria, wanting
to laugh, not daring to.

"A few—a very few—remember. Sadly, there's not much
that can be done for them. It seems that they have an inner
resistance to control. An inner defect."

She found a voice. "Are you going to kill me?"

The mouth opened slightly, as if its owner was appalled.
"I don't kill people, Citizeness."

"What about the boy on the cross? Is he alive?"

The lips smiled—gently, tenderly. "The boy was chosen. He is resurrected."

She tried to swallow, but her mouth was too dry. "That's what you plan for me? Death and resurrection?"

"There is such a preoccupation among immortals about death, isn't there? That's why we have places like this." He laughed softly, "So little faith . . . the chosen ones know. The body is something to shed when the time comes."

"And you're the one to decide on the time."

"People need guidance, Citizeness. But I can see that you're frightened. Don't be. I'm not going to kill you." He stood and said to the two men, "Follow me."

They marched her between them to a dim empty room. He touched a lever and a section of the wall moved away. A stone slab rolled out into the room.

Liss stared at it in horror. A girl lay on the slab. She was nearly nude, covered only with thin veils. Her skin was coated with a waxy film that made her look like tallow in the dim light. "She's dead."

"Oh, no. Not dead at all. She's been given a combination of drugs—one to slow her life processes; the other is a synthesis of the body's own chemicals. She's paralyzed—the same paralysis we all experience each night during REM sleep, when we dream. But of course, she doesn't dream. She's quite aware of us." He ran his hand over her body, "Aren't you, dear?"

Liss felt herself begin to tremble, "Why—why is she here? On that slab?"

A note of surprise entered his voice, "Why, this her work. To give pleasure."

The trembling grew to violent proportions. "Then . . . she's a prostitute."

"I suppose you could call her that. But, it's a service, you see. She was one of those unfortunates who kept remembering. But now, she serves."

He looked at the still figure fondly and caressed her again. "She must be very proud to be of service." He looked at Liss; he smiled. "She's been here for over thirty years."

Chapter 10

Kurt stepped off the skiptor and walked swiftly to the processing area. He carried Michael in his arms. The little boy was asleep, black curly head nestled against Kurt's shoulder. David followed them. As he walked, his infrasound recorder swung in an arc at his waist.

A man stepped up to Kurt. "Mr. Kraus? Citizen Kraus?"

He nodded.

"Message for you, Mr. Kraus."

Kurt snapped it open:

JOIN ME AT ONCE ON THE RAM. . . . . . . .JACOBY.

They were the only passengers on the Ram shuttle, which Kurt had hastily commandeered with a priority code.

They debarked through a pressurized tunnel. At the sublif, they were met by a workman. "Mr. Kraus?"

He nodded.

"You're to meet Jacoby in Central Com. You can follow me." He led them through a maze of passages to a second sublif. "We're not going all the way to Central Hab," said the man. "Most of Communications is in the level below."

They followed in silence. Michael walked beside him, rubbing his eyes with one hand, clinging to Kurt with the other.

A nagging anxiety tormented Kurt, and he could see it

reflected in David's eyes. Where was Liss? What had happened? Jacoby wouldn't have summoned them so urgently unless something had gone wrong.

The sublif opened to a large room. They were in a three-vee studio, partitioned into sections. The room was empty. Their footsteps echoed as they followed the man.

"In here," he said. They had stopped in front of Central Communication's Control Room. The man indicated the door, turned and walked away.

Kurt touched the door. It slid open and the three walked in.

Jacoby sat at the end of a long table. The room was dim. Colored lights winked from control panels flanking him. He sat rigidly, hands tensed on the shiny surface of the table. His face looked strained.

"What's wrong?" Kurt stepped forward. "What's happened to Liss?"

Jacoby stared at him. Between the man's still hands, something flickered on the surface of the table. A reflection. Kurt whirled around.

Tarantino smiled gently back at him. He sat in a padded control chair, one arm thrown casually over its back. Behind him stood two armed men with heavy silver T's around their necks.

"He's got her, Kurt." Jacoby's voice was harsh.

"It was thoughtful of you to send the message to Jacoby," said Tarantino. "I might have overlooked your wife's visit without it."

"Where is she? What have you done?"

Tarantino touched a link of the chain around his neck.

"He's subvocaling," said Jacoby. "The necklace is a transmitter. The others receive. They're no more than zombies."

Tarantino smiled, "Zombies? No. Just a few special subjects." A control screen flashed on.

Kurt stared at the screen. He saw a dim room with rock walls. A tall woman touched a panel and a stone slab glided out from the wall. He saw Liss—a close-up of her face, very still, very pale, with a yellowish cast. The flickering light played over her hair.

He heard David gasp. He heard his own voice, strangely altered, say, "Dead? Liss dead?" She couldn't be. Not dead. Not dead. His hands drew into fists so tight the skin was white over his knuckles, and yet he couldn't move, couldn't take his eyes from the flickering screen.

"No. Not dead," said Tarantino softly.

"Better dead," said Jacoby. "He's got her in the Labyrinth."

Liss? There? He tried to absorb it.

"Bait for the scum of Vesta. Something new to titillate the necrophiliacs." Jacoby spat against the glossy surface of the table.

David's face was very pale in the dimness.

A muscle ticked at the angle of Kurt's jaw. He stared at Tarantino. "What do you want for her? Is it me you want?"

The little man's brows arched quizzically. "But, I have you now, don't I?" He swiveled in his chair and surveyed the group. "I'm taking over the Ram. I planned it all along, you see. I wanted it to be finished, so that the people left on Earth would know it was a symbol of a new order.

Kurt's eyes narrowed, "What do you mean, 'the people left on Earth'?"

"You'll see." His hand touched another link and turned once. A series of screens flashed on.

They looked into the L-5 quarters of the Guardian Force. Colonel Gunnar Holst lounged against thick cushions and watched the latest three-vee transmission from Vesta. He clutched a beer, warming it in his hands.

Silvio's lips barely moved. Only a slight swelling in his throat betrayed his almost silent speech. His hand dropped from the necklace.

As they watched, Holst set down his beer and walked with great deliberateness into the Guardian Force war room. The other man at the monitor looked up as he walked in.

Holst leaned over the man. As he did, he maneuvered the silver T at his throat so that it reflected in the man's eyes. A half-minute passed, and then the two began to move the controls on the console. A red warning light flashed on: TWENTY MINUTES TO TARGET.

"We had a code, you see," said Tarantino mildly.

"Oh Christ!" said Jacoby. "He's got them aimed at Earth. He's going to kill them all. Oh, Christ, oh, Christ."

"But, I wouldn't do that," said the little man. "Not all. This is just a lesson. Very limited. The warheads are aimed only at the Chatlanta Ministry Center and at Renascence."

"Renascence?" David sucked in his breath sharply. "Stoey?"

"It had to be Renascence, don't you see? It isn't run well. The people there do as they please. There's no control." He clasped his hands together. "Without control, they could do anything. Invent anything. It's too dangerous."

Kurt felt himself shaking with rage. With an effort he drew a deep breath and looked sidelong at David. He needed to signal him somehow to turn on the recorder. It was the only chance they had left.

Silvio looked at Kurt thoughtfully. "The boy's recording device is an example of what I mean. The empath effect—" He smiled. "Your wife told me all about it."

Kurt's head jerked back as if he had been struck. Fool, he thought. Fool. Had he really believed that he could fight this man with a recorder and a retarded child? And how? Even if he could try, what good would it do? How would it help to look into the sick, black mind of this man? He had already glimpsed its depths, already seen enough.

And then David said, "I guess you're right to be afraid of it. I guess you wouldn't want anyone to know what's inside of you. You wouldn't dare."

"Wouldn't dare?" Tarantino's brow arched above his black eyes. "You think I'm afraid of your toy?"

"Yes. I do."

The little man looked evenly at him for a few seconds. Then he began to laugh softly. "Turn it on."

David looked at Kurt.

He nodded. The monitor screen flickered across Tarantino's face, red from the warning light flashing in the L-5 war room: SEVENTEEN MINUTES TO TARGET. He took Michael's hand, and as the boy's fingers curled around his, Kurt turned to face Silvio. "Hold the boy's other hand."

With a condescending nod, Silvio enclosed Michael's small hand in his.

"You're too close," David whispered. "I can't narrow the beam enough. You're both in it."

"Turn it on," Kurt said.

As he hesitated, Kurt's gaze locked with his. "Turn it on, David. And no matter what happens, don't shut it off."

With a faint click, the recorder turned on.

Kurt felt the floor open under his feet.

. . . He was falling. It was black and he was falling. Cold. Black.

He tumbled, yawing and spinning, into a vortex that he could not see. There was no sound except the hiss of blood rushing in his ears. No sound. But something. What?

Something.

A low laugh. Again. A voice: "Come in."

A pinpoint of light—a firefly. He spun toward it headlong. He strained to see and saw nothing more than the pinpoint, growing to a fuzzy star.

He fell.

The light grew as he plunged toward it. It erupted suddenly to such a blinding white that he squeezed his eyes tight against it, yet still it seared through his tightly shut eyelids. He wheeled in the darkness. The light tracked him.

He opened his eyes to slits. Cold fire rippled in his belly; the light blazed into a shape—a silver T.

Its surface shone like glass. It was huge and solid. No matter which way he turned, it tracked him.

He felt himself pulled closer. He felt its ice, its fire.

He opened his eyes and looked into the silver surface. The reflection was his own. With a shuddering gasp he realized that he was staring into himself, into what he really was. He reached out and tried to push away this thing that looked into the marrow of his soul . . .

. . . His fingers closed over the gold egg. It was the prize. He added it to his basket. It lay with the others, two blue and a yellow, on a nest of curly green. He toddled over the lawn. Mommy and Daddy stood with the others, talking in a big group. Excited, he began to run toward them.

He tripped over a long root and tumbled onto the hard
ground. His basket flipped on its side; the colored eggs spilled
on the dirt. Blood oozed from his knee.

A hand, larger than his, scooped up the gold egg.

He stared at the bigger boy who stole his egg. "Mine.
Gimme."

The big boy stuck out his tongue.

"Mine." He began to cry.

The bigger boy looked around in alarm. "You better shut
up."

His knee hurt, and he wanted his egg. He cried harder.

"Here's your old egg." The boy smashed it into his face,
crushing it against his nose. Sharp edges of the shell stabbed
in his face and eye. The boy ran. .

. . . SAFETY DAY. Safety, safety, safety . . . "You
kids." . . . The chain sang through the air, wrapping around
his ribs. Hot shocking pain . . . The bike crawled . . .
"Mama. Help me—". . . .

His mama and daddy stood in the room by his crib. They
thought he was asleep. Eric sprawled on the youth bed across
the room. His cowboy blanket was kicked in a heap on the
floor. The nightlight dimmed as his mother passed in front of
it. She picked up the blanket and covered Eric, tucking it in
at the foot.

She came and stood by his crib then. His father looked at
him in the dimness. "We should have stopped with one. We
can't afford him."

"You're just worried. Things will work out," she said.

"I don't know." . . .

. . . "Number one son." Eric grinned in pleasure . . .
should have stopped with one . . . *I wanted to kill you.* . . .

"Don't kill it. Don't. Don't. *Don't.*"

The little bat had fallen from the scarred oak in the school
yard. Its body was soft brown fur; its wings were black leather.
He saw it first. He stared at it in fascination. It lay on its back
and gave out high piping squeaks. The first stone was small.
It struck the little body squarely and the creature screamed in
torment. "Don't," he shrieked.

"We got to."

"Why?"

"Because it's a *bat*."

Another stone struck . . . the chain sang through the air . . . "I hate you, I hate you, I hate you."

"You're weird, Kurt." The girl sucked her ice and stared at him. "Why don't you take human lessons from your brother?" . . .

. . . The second-grade teacher handed out the readers. He sat next to Harriet Seevers. It made him feel strange, sitting next to her. She was big—nearly eleven—and stupid. A re-tard. He hated her. She made him feel sick inside. "Re-tard," he said under his breath, glaring at her, "re-tard." She made him feel scared, like maybe it could happen to him. *I hate you, I hate you, I hate you.* . . .

His fists hammered at nothing. The silver T mocked him. He stared at it and another layer of himself fell away. . . .

He stood on a colorless beach under a blank sky. A silver sea rolled away in front of him. He whirled around. He was on an island. It was tiny, stretching less than his body's length in all directions. He shouted, "Help." And the words turned into glass in the air above him, shattering, raining sharp splinters down on him.

He knelt on the sand, digging frantically. He drew the pile of sand around him, patting it, smoothing it until the wall rose high around him, curving over him. He made it thick and strong, and when it was finished, he made a tiny peephole in the wall and looked out. . . .

The silver keys of his oboe glowed, and as he watched, they dimmed and tarnished. . . .

The wall needed to be thicker. It could crumble. He smoothed the red clay into bricks and placed them carefully. He peeped out. . . .

The clay bank was hung with ferns. Tanya's naked feet made small prints in the clay. She stepped onto a smooth stone. Sun and shadow played on the whiteness of her body. Laughing, she jumped into the rocky pool, squealing at the cold. The water splashed over her breasts and drained in little rivers over her belly.

He heard her music from within his wall. He peeped through and saw her standing in the rock pool, laughing, reaching for him. The wall began to crumble, to fall away, and he stepped from it. She was warm in his arms, warm, then strangely cold in his embrace. Horrified, he stared as she melted away in his arms. He clawed at shadows. . . .

"Daddy, I want." . . . "I need, Daddy." . . . "Stop it, Kurt." . . . "I hate you, Daddy. I wish you was dead." . . . "Daddy? Daddy!". . . .

The silver T turned. He faced it. . . .

He stood on the colorless island. Faces emerged from the silver sea . . . His parents . . . Grandma . . . Eric . . . Tanya . . . A touch of color—Liss—golden hair moving like feathers in the wind, then still. . . . The colors faded. Her face was still and pale as death. . . .

The faces dimmed and blurred. . . .

I'm going to live. I'm going to watch you die.

The faces began to run like quicksilver into the shining black sea. He turned his back on them, but the silver sea mocked him and gave him back his own face. And it was afraid. . . .

He ran toward the golden egg, reaching for it, and as he reached, it turned to silver and grew giant against the blackness. It was the Ram, and he knew it then for what it was— not a goal, it was a hiding place—a place to creep into, a place with thickly curved and nurturing walls. . . .

He lay naked on the tiny island and looked up at a blank sky. "*I'm going to watch you die.*" And he knew that he spoke of himself, of each part of himself he had stifled and denied. He flung the words out and they were stones that fell back, striking him. He tried to move away from the rain of stones, but he couldn't. He had no right to live.

When the last stone fell, it struck his chest, crushing his ribs against his heart. The force of the blow thrust him into the sea. He submerged and drifted downward. He felt quicksilver wash over him and flood his mouth and lungs. He was dying. He felt himself dying and he accepted it. . . .

And then a color came—a blue against a bright white. It swirled and formed a circle, then a globe. Blue. A blue lake. White fluffy clouds reflected in the blueness. Renascence.

Fight.

He couldn't.

Fight.

He must. But he couldn't.

Fight.

He moved his arms. A shriek of pain flooded him. He moved again. His dying body protested. Slowly, painstakingly, he began to swim. . . .

The silver T faced him. He saw himself reflected in it, naked. Wounded, dying, he reached out and touched it.

It moved away.

Struggling, he tried to reach it. As he did, he felt the force behind it, the malevolence of it. He heard it laugh softly.

The laugh gave him resolve. With a lunge, he grasped the silver T. It burned into the flesh of his hands, but he had it now. In pain and triumph he cried, "Look. Look at yourself." And with the last of his strength, he slowly turned the shining weapon in upon its source. . . .

The light of the silver T faced a blackness, an emptiness, so complete that nothing reflected back its light. Clutching it, he plunged into a lonely emptiness so vast he was a speck, an atom, an infinitesimal particle, falling through nothing at all.

Nothing. And that was its horror—and its strength.

He fell endlessly, clutching his burden. He saw nothing. Nothing. . . .

He heard a voice. . . .

"I'm going to name him Silvio. His name is Silvio." . . .

"Scrawny little thing, isn't he?" . . .

Nothing.

. . . *Only thirty minutes remain in the Safety Day grace period. All children—repeat, all children—must be taken at once to the closest receiving station.* . . .

. . . "I know you want the best for your baby, Kitty. That's why we're here . . . It's for his own good." . . .

Then another voice.

"I forgot you again, didn't I, little guy?" . . . "but there are so many." . . .

"I didn't mean to let him lie so long." . . . "—so homely. That birthmark—" . . .

"He'll be back with his mama soon. They can't keep up this safety thing forever."

"Didn't you hear? "A whisper." She killed herself. Turned on the gas." . . .

A light. A tiny light. . . .

He lay in his crib, turning his head, fixing his strange dark eyes on the foot of it. He was wet and cold and his stomach cramped with hunger. He gnawed at his fist.

His infant mind sought survival. Wordless, it sought a focus, a way of control, a source of strength. He stared at the foot of his crib, at the letter that signified his name, his section, in the long rows of cribs filled with crying babies. The T was small and made of aluminum, and when the afternoon rays of the sun struck just right, it looked like silver.

He stared at it, at the great silver T—the power. He began to cry.

And someone came. . . .

The T shriveled and consumed itself, and in a flash winked out. He was left in utter blackness. Bleak winds blew in emptiness . . . emptiness . . . emptiness. . . .

The winds died down to nothing.

Nothing.

Nothing at all. . . .

And then a trickle. The tiniest trickle of something. Something warm and infinitely comforting. He reached out, touched it.

It was another hand; it clasped his.

Kurt stumbled against Michael's grasp. The walls of the communications room reeled. A red light flashed: TWO MINUTE WARNING.

Silvio Tarantino lay on the floor, curled in a fetal ball. He was wet and soiled. He sucked a fist, soaked with his saliva and his tears.

The two armed men stared at him in horror.

With a leap, Jacoby was at Tarantino's side. He jerked the silver T from Tarantino, thumbed a link and frantically subvocaled, "Abort! Abort!"

They stared at the screen. Colonel Gunnar Holst stiffened.

"Abort! Abort!"

Holst stood and walked into the war room. Uncertainly, he faced the other man.

"Abort. For God's sake!" Jacoby's whisper was a scream.

Holst flashed the silver T in the other man's eyes. The seconds rolled by. No one breathed as the two men's hands moved over the console.

The red light flashed.

Then yellow: MISSION ABORTED.

A collective breath went out through the room. Then Jacoby ran his fingers savagely over the links of the necklace. Two dozen screens lit up. Two dozen faces. . . .

Jacoby turned the silver T in his hand. "Now hear this," he bellowed. "This is God. You take off that fucking necklace and throw it in the fucking *trash!*"

Word came by radio that Liss was safe. And with the news, Kurt felt a relief that unwound his nerves and set his legs to trembling with fatigue. He watched as Jacoby's men led Tarantino away. Then David turned to Kurt. "What's going to happen to Silvio now? And the others?"

"It's going to take a long time," said Kurt. A long time and a lot of patience. The Ministry and Vesta had a great deal to work out, he thought. Maybe now, they could.

"I want to tell you something," said David. "I made up my mind about you, without really knowing you. I—" He paused and looked away, then back. "I stood on the edge, back there. It was happening to you, but it happened to me, too. Do you know what I mean?"

Kurt nodded. Beside him, Michael scrubbed his eyes in fatigue. Kurt hoisted him to his shoulder.

David's face grew solemn. "I know what it is to feel different. To feel—pushed out. But I never really thought that anyone else felt that way." He looked down, staring at the gold and black ring he wore for a moment before he said, "I know you love Liss, too. I think you need to tell her so."

Kurt blinked and cleared his throat.

"Are you—Are you going to go away on the Ram? Now that you know—"

"Now that I know I was running away?" asked Kurt softly. The Ram could be a cozy womb, he thought. And it could be more. "The Ram can be a birthplace too, David. Yes. I'll be aboard her. And you?"

Surprise flickered across David's face. "Why, I guess I'll go back to Renascence. It's where I belong." He reached out his hand to Kurt, who clasped it. "Good voyage." He turned to go, then he stopped and said, "At the end, back there, there was something. . . . Something that came into the emptiness. . . ."

Kurt smiled through his fatigue. "It was love, David. It came from this little one." He looked down at the child who clung to him. "It came from Michael."

He sat at her bedside until she woke and saw him there. "Oh, Kurt. It was so awful."

He held her, patted her, as she sobbed. "Oh, Kurt. Don't leave me."

He kissed her then. "Come with me, Liss. I love you."

Chapter 11

Inside the Ram's curving walls, Kurt stood hand-in-hand with Liss in the little park.

"But, Kurt," she protested, "I want to watch from the viewport. If I'm going to keep the Ram's archives, I need to be a witness. Besides," she added, "I want to see."

"Just wait a moment," he said. "Jacoby tells me we'll have time to watch." He smiled. "Trust me."

Her brows rose in mock exasperation. And then from across the green park, something caught her eye. A young woman walked toward them. She carried a child, a very small child, with hair as wild and blonde as Liss's own, with eyes as blue. "Oh, Kurt," she said, "Alani?"

He nodded.

She ran to meet them. Then stopped and stared a moment before she gathered the little girl in her arms. "Oh, baby. Oh, sweet baby."

Alani's eyes were round with delight. She patted Liss's cheek with a chubby hand. "Pretty lady."

"Kurt, what does it mean? Can I keep her?"

He grinned and nodded. They all had a lot of reassessing to do, he thought. They had kept to many ways because they seemed safe: the dormitories, the Ministry. . . . But they weren't safe. They had bred a monster in Silvio, a tragic, pitiable monster. And somewhere along the way they had left out things that mattered like Christmas trees and caring and families, things like finding out what people really wanted.

Her eyes were bright as she looked at him. "You know, I really never thought of her, when I was pregnant. I was thinking of David. And I was thinking of myself, mostly." She stroked Alani's hair. "Secretly, I was feeling noble, giving David his chance at immortality. It was mine, really. The baby was a chance for me to create something. It wasn't until she came—until they took her away—" She began to sob, clutching at the little girl.

Alani touched the wet cheek, then examined in surprise the chubby fingers that came away damp with tears. "Don't cry." Her lower lip slid out and her eyes were round with alarm.

Liss's lips trembled into a smile.

Kurt kissed them both, "Come on," he said. "It's time to say goodbye to the sun."

The Ram gleamed silver in the night of space. She moved off Vesta slowly, very slowly, at first. And tiny ships, dwarfed by her size, flanked her. Skiptors, shuttles, battered freighters followed, flashing their lights on her hull as she glided away from home toward a deeper sea.

And as she moved away, she broadcast music.

The people listened in the Ram and in the farthest reaches of the belt.

On Earth, a small child heard and said, "Oh, what's that?"

"Sh-h-h, listen. Listen to the Earth's song."

It played in places without names; it played in the largest cities. And at the speed of light it sent its song into the depths of space.

Kurt stood with his little family and watched through the transparent viewport walls. The stars were very bright.

He looked around him at the throng of people, some strangers, some old friends. Little Michael was there, and the children who would enter New Renascence. They listened to the song as Earth itself slipped away. It's what we are, he thought. "Earth Song" swelled into its climax, and tears sprang to eyes that tried for one last glimpse of home.

And then the Ram's star drive burst into life and thrust

them outward bound. Earth's song preceded them. We're coming, it announced. From Earth. And this is what we are. Who would hear? he wondered. Who would listen?